REIGN OF THE DESERT WOLF

ALPHA

RED ROCK PACK
BOOK 1

JD WOLFE

Reign Of The Desert Wolf
Copyright © 2024 JD Wolfe

To request permissions, contact the publisher at
unleashed@jdwolfebooks.com
Paperback: ISBN: 979-8-9919512-1-0

Note from Author
This is a work of fiction. Unless otherwise indicated, all the names, characters, businesses, places, events, and incidents in this book are either the product of the author's imagination or used in a fictitious manner. Any resemblance to actual persons, living or dead, or actual events is purely coincidental.

First Edition June 2023
Second Edition December 2024
Third Edition December 2025

Cover Design by JD Wolfe
jdwolfebooks@gmail.com
jdwolfepack.com

Another Note From the Author Because She Likes
Words:

This book contains; violence, abuse, blood, gore, murder, and a mention of
the devil. It also describes in detail sexual acts and nudity. As well as every
known cuss word with some new made-up ones.

"For the ones who'd rather run with wolves than deal with humans."

"To Hubs, who's proof that sometimes the perfect mate isn't found, but made."

CONTENTS

Red Rock Pack

CONFIDENTIAL

Council of
the Animal Society

Threat Level
1 2 3 ④ 5

CONFIDENTIAL

Name: Randolph, Charlotte

Pack: Red Rock Pack

Pack Position: Alpha

DOB: M 11 | D 11 | Y 81 **Age:** 42

Registered Animal: Wolf

US Citizen: Yes **Language:** English

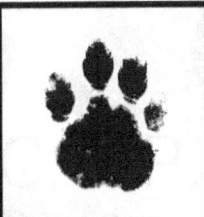

Height	5'10"
Weight	120
Hair Color	Black
Eye Color	Green
Skin Tone	Medium

Pack Information

Mate: Dunne, Liam

Beta: Sheridan, Harper

Enforcer: Devereaux, Jade

Pack: Unknown

Registered Address:
117 Stanley Dr
Lake Las Vegas, NV

Psychological Profile:

- Highly intelligent and strategic
- Trained in combat, extremely dangerous when provoked
- Loyal to her pack—will do anything to protect them
- Strong anti-authority tendencies

Threat Level

1 2 3 ④ 5

| File Number | #95423975-17 |
| Shifter ID Code | #W122581-F |

Intended for Official Use Only.

CONFIDENTIAL

Name: Dunne, Liam

Pack: Former Ashland Pack

Pack Position: Lone Wolf

DOB: | M 02 | D 18 | Y 79 | **DOB:** 43

Registered Animal: Wolf

US Citizen: Yes **Language:** English

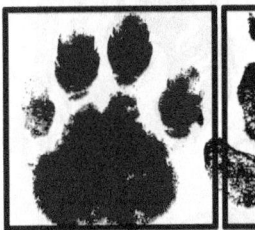

Height	6'5"
Weight	235
Hair Color	Brown
Eye Color	Brown
Skin Tone	Olive

Pack Information

Registered Address:
Unknown

Mate: Deceased

Alpha: Lone Wolf Status

Beta:

Enforcer:

Psychological Profile:

- Exhibits strong protective instincts toward vulnerable individuals
- Avoidant of personal conflict but extremely capable when provoked
- Uses logic and routine as stabilizers
- Shows minimal ego; prioritizes group safety over personal status

MOVING DAY

Moving day has finally arrived.

Finding a house for four opinionated, strong-willed she-wolves?

Harder than herding cats.

Charlotte exhales, jaw tight. Of course it is. Even the universe loves mocking her with puns.

They've scoured every corner of the city, considering everything from Spanish-style villas to sleek modern homes, with debates over pools, no pools, and—seriously— what the hell is a barndominium?

If they can survive picking out a home together, they can survive anything.

Charlotte stands outside, gazing up at the ten-bedroom Mediterranean-style mansion on Lake Las Vegas. It's way more than they need, but when you work as hard as these bitches do, you deserve to splurge a little.

The elaborate split staircase with a fountain in the center screams, "Hey, look at me!"—a perfect reflection of their larger-than-life personalities.

But really, who in the hell is going to clean all those windows? Even the five garage doors have mirrored fronts.

Luna, with her ever-present sense of humor, has already dubbed the perfectly trimmed palm trees lining the driveway her "Vegas Autobahn."

But it's the backyard that sealed the deal—the grotto pool and three hot tubs pushed them all over the edge.

Walking up the driveway, Charlotte notices the female moving crew closing the backdoor of the hot pink truck. Each side is emblazoned with white block lettering:

How Many Girls Does It Take Moving Company.

The name alone won them the job. She hands an envelope to the blonde in the driver's seat, dressed like a modern-day Rosie the Riveter.

"Thanks, ladies. I'll add a good review in a couple of days, and there's a little extra in there for you." Charlotte taps the window frame with a grin before heading toward the front door.

Stepping into the grand, eclectically decorated foyer, Charlotte's gaze lands on the gold and black compass inlay on the floor. The intricate design reminds her that no matter which direction she chooses, she'll always find her way back to her pack.

Planting her feet firmly, she takes a deep breath. This house is a lot—over the top, even—but with the increasing threats from the Cascade Pack, she needs to do everything in her power to keep her sisterhood safe. This mansion provides room to grow, though she's not quite ready to have those conversations yet.

The Red Rock Pack is a rare breed in the shifter world. An all-female pack that once thrived in safety through sheer numbers.

Charlotte, Harper, and Jade found others like them,

growing the pack to fifteen. But now, only Luna remains alongside the original three.

Luna's initiation had been under difficult circumstances, but they need her just as much as she needs them.

Holding onto their territory has become increasingly dangerous with just the four of them, but their bonds are strong, and they'll fight to the death to keep what's theirs.

Charlotte steps into the white gothic-inspired kitchen, where the other three ladies are gathered around a large gold-veined black marble island.

They're all picking at an elaborate charcuterie board. Charlotte's pretty sure Harper "threw" it together, even though it looks fit for royalty. She reaches for a piece of cheese—pauses—and realizes she has no idea what the hell Luna is talking about now.

Luna looks otherworldly in that way only she can pull off. Alabaster skin. Snow-white hair women spend fortunes trying to fake. Those ridiculous purple eyes that glow against her pale complexion. She's small for a wolf shifter, almost fragile-looking, but Charlotte knows better. Under all that softness is a beast fierce enough to make demons think twice. And that sly smile of hers? Pure trouble.

"The fact that life, as in proton and electron formation, exists for only a billionth of a billionth of a billionth of the time the universe will exist—events continue to happen. At the end of that timescale, they theorize proton decay will occur. So, literally, nothing will ever happen...forever. Entropy is inevitable. I think it's wild to consider that the universe will end in ice."

"Luna, what in the actual fuck are you talking about?" Jade says, her confusion lines deepening into canyons. "I asked if you were happy that we have an ice maker now."

Luna shrugs, nonchalant as ever. "Fine. Yes, I am excited that we have an ice maker now."

"Speaking of having new things," Harper chimes in, her voice as smooth as the silk scarf tied around her neck, "does anyone object to me changing the backsplash? I came across these teal octagon tiles, and they would look so hot in this kitchen."

All three women shake their heads in unison.

"The kitchen is yours. None of us cook, so go wild," Jade says, snatching a fancy cracker topped with some obscure cheese and popping it into her mouth.

The charcuterie board isn't your average salami-and-cheddar affair. One of the fruits looks like something straight out of *cartoon*, and there are at least five different cheeses with varying degrees of stink. Charlotte's pretty sure this spread came straight from France. The caviar is served with a tiny spoon, surrounded by an artful display of crackers. But what catches Charlotte's eye is something small and round.

"Are these real fucking honeycombs, Harper? This shit is too beautiful to eat," she says, chewing on a slice of Soppressata.

Harper hands Charlotte a mason jar filled with clear bubbly. "We waited so we could toast to the Red Rock Oasis."

"Red Rock Oasis?" Charlotte raises an eyebrow at Luna.

Luna's mischievous smile spreads across her face. "I wanted to call it Red Rock Asylum, but apparently that doesn't promote the *ray of fucking sunshine* we're living under now."

Charlotte can't help the snort.

"What?" Now, all three of them are staring at her expectantly.

As Alpha, they look to her for a brilliant, heartfelt toast about how this house will make them stronger, about how they'll face the future together, *blah, blah, blah.* But Charlotte is more of a "just do it" kind of gal, not one for flowery speeches.

She rolls her eyes. "Okay, fine. Hold up your damn glasses. It's taken us years of tears, sweat, and literal blood, but we're finally in the same den with room to grow. Those of us who are left will be stronger for it. RIP to the ones we've lost, and for us...cheers to not dying."

Three pairs of eyes widen as if they might pop out of their heads before the room erupts in laughter. In stereo, the three women echo, "Cheers to not dying."

THE REASON WE CAN'T
HAVE NICE THINGS

Charlotte spends the afternoon unpacking her clothes and meticulously arranging her new, swanky bathroom—marble gleaming in every direction, a rain shower big enough to fit questionable choices, and towels so thick they could insulate a small cabin.

The moment she saw the place, she knew it was hers—especially the spa tub, which she intends to claim tonight.

She steps into the shower, its ridiculous size perfect for, say, half the local hockey team. A grin flicks at her lips. Hmm. Tempting

As the water cascades down her bronzed gym-toned body, she hopes her sisters are finding the same solace in their own spaces.

If the four of them can create sanctuaries within their individual spaces, perhaps their inner beasts will finally stop growling and tearing at their chests from the inside-out.

Lathering up the pink soap on her pouf, a wave of

sadness suddenly washes over her. The broken bonds of her lost sisters weigh heavily on her heart.

The Red Rock Pack has battled with tooth and claw to defend their territory, and it has cost them nine of their sisters.

What began as their desert sanctuary has become a battleground for vengeance, thanks to that narcissistic penis-wrinkle, Miles Barlowe, Alpha of the Cascade Pack.

"Nope," she mutters, shaking her head, refusing to go down that dark road.

Stepping out of the shower, smelling like a damn garden and wrapped in a towel, she looks around her very large master suite. A smile, that she can't stop, creeps across her face. Her wolf, usually a restless beast growling at anything and everything, is quiet–content even. *This is a good sign.*

Luca and Wesley, her interior designers who are as beautiful as they are talented, knew exactly how to create her space. The extra-large bed, nearly the size of a small boat, fills the room–a bit eccentric for Charlotte's taste, but it's like sleeping on a fucking cloud. They called the overall design "simple elegance."

It's more than Charlotte ever imagined for herself, but the teal overstuffed couch and the 65-inch TV will come in handy for those inevitable sunup to sundown marathons.

She pulls on her favorite purple tank top, and an internal growl that isn't her wolf, catches her attention. The box of Flavor Blast Goldfish she stashed in the back of the pantry suddenly sounds like the best idea she's ever had.

Easing the door open, she steps into the hallway, her gaze sweeping over the long stretch of white walls adorned with vibrant modern art. That was all Harper. *Boujee bitch.*

Each piece seems to pulse with energy, *those designers know their shit.*

The hallway extends endlessly, doors spaced evenly along both sides like sentinels guarding hidden secrets. There must be at least fifteen of them, each holding the promise of something yet to be discovered.

Across from her, Harper's suite lies open, the doorway showing a beautiful light blue, beckoning her to step inside. The familiar hum of music floats out, mingling with the air, but Charlotte hesitates, feeling an unspoken boundary. *That's new.*

"Harper?" Charlotte calls, poking her head into the doorway.

They've been crammed together for so long that it feels almost wrong to enter Harper's space without permission.

The only response is the faint sound of Taylor Swift somewhere in the room.

Charlotte backs out and continues downstairs, her thoughts firmly on those Goldfish.

As she turns the corner into the kitchen, she discovers why Harper didn't answer her call at the doorway. Hearing an edge in Harper's voice.

"Luna, that is not fucking spaghetti. I don't care what the sauce is or what the label says."

Charlotte saunters over to the custom-designed six-burner stove, where Luna is calmly stirring something in a pot, the rich aroma of tomatoes and spices filling the air. "What are you doing now, besides pissing Harper off?" she asks, a smirk tugging at the corner of her lips.

Luna's hand moves in a steady rhythm, her face an unruffled mask of serenity as the thick red sauce swirls around tiny, circular noodles.

"Luna apparently made, 'quote unquote' spaghetti for everyone," Harper announces, her fingers punctuating the air with exaggerated quotes. Her voice drips with disdain.

"But it's fucking SpaghettiOs, Luna." She spits out Luna's name like it's something bitter she needs to expel.

"Harper! It literally has spaghetti in the name, so that makes it spaghetti!" Luna counters, her tone an exasperated mix of amusement and logic.

Harper's eyes narrow as she fires back, "Yes, and that phone sitting next to you is an Apple, but that doesn't mean you can take a bite out of it."

"Ooooooo, mic drop," Jade chimes in, the tight twists in her hair bouncing as she spins on the barstool. Her dark eyes glint with appreciation for Harper's quick wit.

Charlotte rolls her eyes, feeling the tension in the room building like a storm ready to break. "Ladies! Remember the deal. Fights go outside. We bought a house with white tile like fucking morons," her voice edged with a touch of Alpha power to make sure they listen.

Both women turn towards the back patio, their argument still simmering as they debate the validity of SpaghettiOs as real spaghetti.

These women are fighters, each with a beast lurking beneath the surface.

Luna's usual mischievous kindness is a mask–one that slips when she's provoked, revealing a side so fierce that even the devil himself would bow before her and her beasts.

As their voices fade into the distance, Charlotte catches Luna's parting shot. "Why do you have to be such a well-done steak, Harper?"

"Again? What the fuck does that even mean, Luna?"

"Well-done steaks annoy me." The door slams behind them, cutting off the last of the argument.

"They're the reason we can't have nice things," Jade mutters, shaking her head as she disappears through the arched doorway leading into the diningroom.

Charlotte glances over both shoulders, then shrugs. With two of the ladies outside likely bleeding each other and the other one off to lose herself in TV, she finds herself alone with a steaming pan of SpaghettiOs.

And look... meatballs!

FUCKING MALES

The next day, Charlotte is strolling past the cardio area of the gym floor, her pace unhurried as she mentally checks off her to-do list.

Suddenly, she halts mid-step, her body going rigid as an unfamiliar scent hits her like a freight train.

It's not the usual assault of sweat and gym-rat testosterone that fills the air; this is different—something softer, something that soothes the edges of her frayed nerves.

Her nostrils flare as she tries to draw in more of the fragrance that is bold and grounding, a mix of redwood and fresh pine, with a smoky edge that hinted at a campfire burning somewhere in the distance. And to her surprise, her wolf, usually a restless force, rolls over, exposing her belly in submission.

What the fuck is that?

Shaking her head, dismissing it as some new deodorant. Probably that one that keeps popping up on her Instagram feed for no damn reason-the one with the catchy slogan, "Men, wash your balls," followed by a montage of soccer balls, basketballs, and other bouncy spheres jumping around the screen.

Fucking brilliant, she thinks with a smirk.

Eyes sweep over the gym, scanning for the source of the scent that has her beast on edge.

Treadmills whirr beneath hunched bodies, and the usual gym bros grunt as they spot each other at the bench press.

Nothing out of the ordinary. No one stands out. With a frustrated sigh, she wonders what the hell is wrong with her beast but decides to let it go.

She drags herself toward the glass-top desk she's always hated. *Seriously, who thought that was a good idea?*

Glancing down, her scowl deepens at the sight of the notifications on her phone. Three missed calls from Luna and one from Jade.

Her irritation simmers as she presses the call button. The moment the line connects, she can feel Luna's panic radiating through the phone. "What the fuck, Luna? Are you okay?"

"Char, I just saw Ethan. I went to the Summerlin house to check that all the windows and doors were locked, and he was creeping around in the backyard. I was careful not to let him know I was there. I didn't want to go beasty, so I left and called you right away."

"Shit," Charlotte mutters, her frustration shifting to their enemy. "Text Jade and tell her to be home by six. I'll get ahold of Harper. Pack meeting."

She stops, rubbing a hand through her hair, tension firing through every stiff movement.

"I'm sure Ethan's already checked the other houses by now. Dammit. I was hoping for peace a little longer."

Luna's voice comes through the phone—steady, but with a crack Charlotte doesn't miss.

"Peace is overrated anyway."

Charlotte freezes. There's something under that tone, something tight.

A beat. Then Luna adds, quieter, more guarded,

"But... with the extra space, maybe it's time to think about bringing in a few more wolves. We need to grow our numbers again."

Charlotte tightens her grip on the phone. Silence stretches between them, heavy with the weight of what Luna isn't saying.

The suggestion feels like a gamble, and Charlotte knows it. She hears it in the way Luna's voice falters, as if she's already bracing for the pushback.

"I know it's a risk, especially after everything," Luna adds softly. "But we can't afford to stay small forever."

Charlotte's heart feels the weight of responsibility, pressing down on her. "Let's talk about it tonight."

Ending the call, Charlotte lets out the long breath she'd been holding. Stopping just short of slamming her fist into the stupid glass desk.

"Why can't they just stay in their own damn territories?"

Harper, Jade, and she created the Red Rock Pack as a sanctuary for females seeking refuge, protection.

Something like an ally pack—the Black Canyon Pack had done for them so many years ago.

They were given food, protection, and training, ensuring their survival.

At its peak, the Red Rock sisterhood was fifteen strong, but battles to save their territory had taken its toll.

Now, it was just the four of them, clinging to their hard-won city of Las Vegas and the surrounding desert. Mourning the loss of their sisters has been difficult for the four remaining Red Rocks.

Charlotte instinctively pulls the hair tie from her jet-black hair, her fingers tugging at it as if the small rubber band itself is the source of the tension coiling inside her.

The wolf within her stirs, restless and growly, pacing at the edges of her mind.

She lets her jet-black hair fall loose, cascading over her shoulders, and promptly begins gathering the strands back into a bun.

Mid-motion, that scent drifts toward her again, soft and familiar, wrapping around her like a soothing whisper.

Her wolf pauses, alert, as the calming fragrance teases both her senses and the beast inside her, pulling them both from the restless spiral of thoughts.

Charlotte glances out the office window, her eyes drifting over the gym floor. Humans pound away on treadmills, sweat flying as their feet strike in rhythmic, almost desperate motions.

Over by the mirrors, the gym bros are at it again, flexing and grinning at their reflections like they're auditioning for a role only they can see.

In the back, neon lights pulse from the spin class, casting an odd glow over the room. The instructors shout encouragement over the blaring music, and the participants pedal furiously, as if trying to outrun something.

Even after years as a trainer, she still doesn't get it-what's so appealing about pretending you're biking through a rave? But then again, what's one woman's pain is another woman's pleasure... or sometimes both.

I need to find the source of that smell.

It's like meditation on steroids, soothing her anxiety in a way nothing else does.

She makes her way to the gym's main room, Britney's "Work B**ch" blaring through the speakers. The scent has faded, but she's determined to track it down.

As she circles the floor, checking in with clients, she tries to catch even a hint of that addictive fragrance, but it eludes her.

With a resigned shrug, she decides she better listen to Britney and "get to work, bitch."

LATER THAT NIGHT, Charlotte waves her hand over the flickering blue flames of the standalone water vapor fireplace. The sleek, modern unit stands close to the windows, its design allowing light and shadow to dance freely around it.

She circles it slowly, the cool mist disguised as fire licking at her palm without heat.

Beyond the glass, the desert night stretches endlessly, but it's the worry etched on her sisters' faces that holds her attention, grating on her nerves.

One day.

They got one fucking day of happiness. The thought burns hotter than the illusionary flames ever could. Charlotte is beyond done—she wants blood.

"Okay, ladies, we knew the Cascade Pack wouldn't leave us alone for long. We bruised their egos, and after the last battle, their numbers are down. But they know ours are too, so I'm sure Ethan was doing some recon for that wrinkled ball sack, Miles."

It was men like Miles who had driven this all-female pack together in the first place.

"Oh, he's just pissed off because everyone knows you, a

female, gave him that limp," Jade says with a smirk, pride gleaming in her eyes.

Old shifter laws were crafted to keep females controlled, subjugated under the guise of order. If a beating was deemed necessary, it was considered perfectly acceptable, well within a male's rights.

Even now, some Alphas still cling to those outdated laws, ruling their packs through fear and brutality.

Miles is one of them. He controls his pack with an iron fist, his leadership steeped in an abusive patriarchy that feeds off dominance and submission.

The scar Charlotte left on him only fueled his twisted sense of power, a constant reminder of the threat strong females pose to his fragile control. It deepened his need to crush any sign of rebellion, to enforce the old ways even more ruthlessly.

The males in his pack follow his lead, emboldened by his rage, while the females live in constant fear, silenced by the ever-present threat of punishment.

"Well, the cuntsickle had it coming. He's lucky that weasel, Ethan, dragged him out of there or his heart would've been a lawn ornament.," Charlotte says, her tone hard as steel.

Jade leans over the hot pink pool table, her fingers steady as she lines up her shot with practiced ease. "Alpha, we need to talk about recruiting," she says, her voice low but firm. "I know the broken bonds are hard for you-they're killing us too-but we can't hold Vegas with these numbers."

Pop.

The cue ball cracks against its target, the sound echoing through the large game room.

Jade straightens, watching the ball sink into the pocket.

"We're badasses, no doubt, but we're all tired. Healing is slower now... harder. We can't keep running on empty."

Charlotte knows Jade is right. Her back has been stiff every morning lately, and just the other day, she noticed a bruise lingering far too long—over five hours for something that should've healed in minutes.

The weight of the broken bonds drags at her, dulling the connection between her and her wolf. The darkness lurking in the distance feels closer with each passing day, like an unwelcome shadow that won't leave.

Glancing at Luna and Harper, curled up on the fluffy white sectional that wraps around most of the room, they look just as worn, their energy dulled.

"Okay," she says, finally nodding. "I'm listening. How do we fix this?" Her voice softens, admitting the need for more bodies, more strength and maybe the chance to heal the hurt inside her.

"We need more of us, no question. But females aren't exactly lining up to join. Who wants to leave one abusive pack just to come here and fight another battle?" She forces a laugh, trying to lift the heaviness in the room. "Plus, our kind of crazy isn't for everyone." Charlotte flashes a teasing smirk at Harper. "I mean, Harper's a bitch."

"Hey!" Harper protests, feigning offense.

Gracefully, Charlotte pours two fingers of whiskey into a cobalt-blue rocks glass—once a wine bottle, now it's adorned with a picture of Old Faithful in white paint.

Swirling the amber liquid thoughtfully before asking, "What do we do, run a Craigslist ad?"

"This is me! This is what I do, Char. I'll work my magic. There are other ladies out there with a badassery level of nine and a half who need a pack. I'll find them," Luna says confidently, her fingers already flying across the keys of her laptop, its lid covered in a chaotic mix of colorful stickers, each one a little piece of her personality.

Sensing there's more on Harper's mind. "Any other suggestions, Harp?"

"What if," Harper begins cautiously, her hands raised in a gesture of surrender, "hear me out—what if we recruit females *AND* males?"

Charlotte is pretty sure Luna's gasp could be heard on the California coast.

"You good?" Jade asks, jabbing a finger toward Luna, her eyes narrowing with concern.

Luna's white hair shimmies down her back as she shakes her head in disbelief. "What the fuck, Harper? Warn a girl before you ram her up the bootyhole."

Charlotte shakes her head, trying to recover from the shock as Harper's suggestion lingers in the air. Her voice wavers, as if testing the very idea on her tongue. "Okay... it's not like we've ever laid down rules about males," she says slowly. "But we've never really talked about it either."

A tightness coils in her stomach, growing heavier as the reality sinks in. The thought of trusting males-letting them into their circle, into the bonds they share-feels foreign, almost dangerous. They've never dared to consider it, not after everything they've been through.

"I'm not sure we're all ready to trust them," she murmurs, the words softer now, haunted by memories she can't quite shake.

Charlotte shifts her almond eyes to Luna, whose scars run deeper than anyone can see. Abused. Tested on. Broken down like some expendable experiment. The walls around Luna's heart aren't just high-they're impenetrable.

Charlotte almost misses the flicker of something—pain, distrust—that crosses Luna's face. It vanishes as quickly as it appeared, hidden behind the playful, lighthearted mask Luna usually wears as her armor. But Charlotte catches it, feels it ripple through their bond. That fleeting crack in her defenses speaks louder than words: this isn't just a new idea —it's a threat to everything they've fought to protect.

"Okay, it was a silly suggestion. I just thought it might be easier and faster to build our numbers if we looked outside the box. Forget I said it," Harper says, her voice tinged with reluctance.

"No, it's worth considering, but we can't rush into this one. We need numbers, but letting males into our bonds isn't as easy as it sounds."

As Charlotte wrestles with the weight of Harper's suggestion, her thoughts drift to the women who have stood by her through countless battles, both physical and emotional. These women are more than just pack members —they are her sisters, each bringing something unique and vital to their tight-knit group. In moments like this, Charlotte can't help but reflect on what makes each of them irreplaceable.

Jade is the type to fuck around and find out, always ready to dive headfirst into danger without a second thought.

Luna, on the other hand, is the masked genius, harboring demons that none of them can imagine.

And then there's Harper, the problem solver, the one who stays level-headed when the rest of the world seems to be spinning out of control.

That's why Charlotte trusts her judgment, but this idea– this radical shift in their pack's dynamic–will take time to process.

"Let's table it for now. Luna, you'll put out some feelers to see if there are any females who want to join a pack of workaholic women on the brink of war with other shifters over a hot, dusty city of sin?"

"Hey, don't forget we're friendly as fuck," Luna snorts. "Well, Harper and I are. Charlotte, you're alright," she says, flipping her hand back and forth dismissively. "Jade... stop biting people."

"I can't help it. People suck, and they deserve it," Jade retorts with a grin.

Charlotte turns back to the group, her gaze sharp. "Let's go see if we can figure out what exactly that asshole was doing at our house and what information he might have taken back to pencil-dick Miles Barlowe."

Luna jumps up, her eyes gleaming with excitement. "Then, Pinkbox Donuts!"

"CHARLOTTE, I know you wanted to make a statement, but did your statement have to be so fucking tall?" Harper grumbles as she hauls herself into the jacked-up TRX, her feet barely scraping the running board.

"Hey, I can't help it if you're a 'fun-sized' wolf," Charlotte shoots back, glancing over her shoulder with a self-satisfied grin.

This badass truck had been her dream for years, and now it was her escape when the girls were being particularly annoying.

The purple ombre paint job gleamed in the sunlight, daring anyone to question her choice. When life got too intense, Charlotte would take this titan into the desert, hitting every bump and rut she could find, letting the rough terrain match her mood.

From the back seat, Luna chimes in, "Oh, I almost forgot

to tell you! My brother called–his wife had the pups, and get this... it was triplets! How wild is that?"

Jade, riding shotgun, slaps her leg and laughs. "Holy shit. They went through the whole pregnancy thinking there were only two, but surprise–three!?"

"Yeah, Jon said the third baby was much smaller and was hiding behind Baby A and Baby B the entire time," Luna explains, a note of awe in her voice.

"What are their names?" Charlotte asks, catching Luna's gaze in the rearview mirror.

"Noah, Bryson, and Ava. Two boys and a teeny little girl. Jon's over the moon. I couldn't be more proud of him–it's like he's finally getting his happy ending. If anyone deserves it, it's Jon," Luna trails off, turning to look out the window. Her eyes narrow suddenly. "Ew, who the fuck ruins a perfectly good Lambo with racing stripes?" Her face scrunching up in disgust. "Idiots with tiny wieners, that's who. Damn, mine looks way better."

Recognizing Luna's deflection, Charlotte knows she needs to gauge where her friend's head is really at.

"How's Jon doing?" she asks, her voice carefully casual. Luna and her twin brother Jon share a past that would haunt most people's nightmares. As Charlotte clicks on the blinker and takes the exit off the freeway, she presses gently, "I mean, aside from the new dad glow?"

"He's good. Found his true mate, can't stop talking about her. The restaurant's doing well, he really likes his in-laws, and now he's got three pups. It's like everything's finally falling into place for him. His happiness was contagious over the phone. I think I'll head up there once things cool off here. I want to meet my nephews and niece."

Charlotte hears the clicks of Harper's fingers dancing across her phone screen, a small smile playing on her lips as she adds items to her online cart at lightning speed. "And you should," she says, not missing a beat. "I'll make sure you've got the cutest basket for those babies." A sudden burst of excitement lights up her face. "Oh my god, look at this!" She turns her phone toward Luna, revealing a tiny onesie with the words *Don't Kiss Me If I Nacho Baby*.

Luna's eyes soften as she leans forward, a hint of hesitation in her movements. Her grin is tentative, almost shy, as she glances at Jade. "Would you... um, would you come with me?" she asks, her voice quieter, as if testing the waters.

"Fuck yeah, I'll go with you." Jade's response is immediate and warm, as she reaches over to press a gentle kiss to Luna's forehead.

Silence settles in the SUV.

Charlotte's mind flickers to the morning she finally walked away.

Her father had hit her before. Many times.

Michael ruled the Sidney Pack like a tyrant, and she'd learned exactly how to read the danger in his voice—the shift in tone, the way the air tightened, the promise of violence.

But that day... it was the words that landed harder than his hand.

"You will do as I say. You will mate with Charles, and you will produce offspring. It's the only fucking thing your side of the species is good for."

She remembers the dirt, the sting, the burn in her spine when she took the uppercut after telling him no.

It wasn't the pain that broke her. It was knowing he would never stop. Charles was the same kind of man. The same kind of cage.

And Charlotte had already decided she would never live her life for a male again.

Sometimes defiance is the only way out. But once a woman finds her strength, it's not defiance anymore. It's who she was always meant to be. And some call that a problem.

As they pull into the driveway of the Summerlin house, Charlotte's is pulled back to the now and her focus sharpens.

The modest, single-story home blends into the neighborhood-just another typical Las Vegas house with its stucco walls and red-tiled roof. A two-car garage sits to the side, and a small patch of desert landscaping lines the front yard, dotted with a few hardy shrubs.

This was one of the three houses the pack called home, a temporary refuge as they built their careers and saved enough to buy one den for them all.

"Jade, take the garage. Luna and Harper, check the bedrooms."

They each head in different directions, moving with the fluidity only a shifter can possess.

Charlotte slips through the side gate into the backyard, her senses on high alert. Her wolf sharpens her instincts. She scans the area, her super-scenting abilities working overtime, searching for any trace of another wolf's scent or any sign of a break-in. Her movements are silent, stealthy—her wolf helping her blend effortlessly into the surroundings, unnoticed by anyone who might be watching.

A few minutes later, Jade's voice rings out, "Nothing is out of place in the garage." She walks through the adjoining door into the kitchen.

Charlotte slides open the glass door from the backyard. "Everything's fine out there. The only scent I picked up is Ethan's."

Luna and Harper return from the hallway, both giving

thumbs up. "No signs of anything off in the bedrooms, and no new smells," Harper reports. "He must have stayed outside. With the shades up, he probably figured out we've moved on."

"Agreed, but now that piece of shit will send scouts to track us down," Charlotte growls softly.

"I think we should drive by the other two houses, just to be sure nothing stands out there," Harper suggests, her voice steady.

"Good call, Harper." Charlotte pivots sharply, her boots barely making a sound on the tile kitchen floor as she heads for the front door, her posture tense and purposeful.

When the pack first made Vegas their home, they had little to no money. They scrounged together just enough for a down payment on a modest house in Lone Mountain. It was cramped, but they made it work, adapting to the harsh desert heat. As their numbers grew, they bought a second house, and at the peak of their strength, the third. The Summerlin house was the last one they needed to sell.

As they back out of the driveway, Luna giggles, "It's a damn miracle we didn't kill each other living in that house."

"We came close a few times," Jade smirks, turning in her seat to look at Luna. "If it weren't for Charlotte, you'd be hobbling around on one leg. We heal fast, but limbs don't grow back." Jade throws Luna a playful wink, her almost-black eyes glinting with mischief. "Remember when you filled my room with thousands of stuffed pigs? Pigs of every size crammed into every corner—you even glued some to the ceiling, for fuck's sake."

"Come on, Jade. It's only because you're the biggest and baddest wolf I know." Luna struggles to keep a straight face but fails miserably, bursting into laughter.

"We had good times in that house," Harper chimes in,

scrolling through her phone once again. She holds up the screen, displaying a picture of the four of them in front of the house, taken the day before they signed the papers for their new den. Even Jade was smiling.

"We've gone through some shit, ladies, but you know what?" Charlotte's voice hardens with determination. "Even the devil is about to find out you don't trifle with the Red Rock Pack."

THE TASTE OF BLOOD

Sitting at her stupid glass desk, Charlotte presses the phone to her ear, patience wearing thin.

"Okay. Yeah, we'll accept that offer...

Yes, Phil, we know it's lower than asking, but it's a young family just trying to make it.

Yeah, all four of us are on board."

She smirks, thinking about Harper's reaction-crying over the letter and those crayon drawings.

"Come on, Phil, don't be such a cold-hearted bitch," she mutters with a grin, rolling her eyes.

"Yes, we'll also take care of the new pool fence and closing costs... Yeah. Yup, that date works for us. Thanks, Phil."

With a quick flick of her fingers, she types out a text to the other ladies.

> I just confirmed with Phil that we accept the family's offer. We'll be paying for the safety fence around the pool and covering closing costs.

Her phone buzzes almost instantly with three replies: two heart emojis and a,

> Fuck yeah!!! Paying it forward 👍

from Jade.

Charlotte's stomach growls, a low rumble that echoes her own growing hunger. *Tacos. Definitely tacos,* she thinks, her mouth already watering at the thought.

"See you tomorrow, Chuck," she calls out with a casual wave as she strides out of Black Wolf Health and Fitness's double doors.

The evening air hits her, cool and crisp, but there's something else—a strange sensation that prickles at the edge of her awareness, like an itch she can't quite scratch. Her steps slow, a sense of unease creeping into her mind. Something is off.

She's halfway to her truck when the little hairs on the back of her neck stand at attention, her wolf stirring with a low growl of warning.

The air feels heavier now, thick with an unidentifiable tension, as if it's charged with electricity that hasn't yet found its release.

Over the years, Charlotte has learned to trust these instincts—they've pulled her back from the brink more than once, and she's not about to ignore them now.

Her sharp eyes dart from shadow to shadow, scanning the parking lot with the precision of a predator. But nothing looks out of place. Yet there's a scent—faint, campfire, threading its way through the air. It's familiar in a way that tugs at the edge of her memory, but also foreign enough to set her nerves on edge. It calms her wolf, lulling it into a false sense of security, but at the same time, it unsettles her human side.

What the hell is this? She draws in a deep breath through her nose, trying to pinpoint the source, but it remains maddeningly elusive, like a whisper she can't quite catch.

Then, like a switch flipping, the tension spikes, the campfire scent pushed to the back of her senses. Five silhouettes materialize, something old and feral stirs in her chest —Black Canyon conditioning. The pack that gave her sanctuary when she had nothing left, the same pack that broke her down and rebuilt her into a weapon. Max's voice flashes in her mind. Lyla's command. The bruises she earned and the strength she claimed.

They made her a war beast.

And now?

These assholes are about to find out exactly what that means.

Her wolf howls within her, muscles coiling with the instinct to defend, to protect what's hers. The air around them crackles with impending violence, and Charlotte feels the familiar surge of adrenaline as her instincts sharpen.

If it means blood, so be it. As the figures draw closer, she narrows her gaze, recognition sparking in her mind the moment the foul stench hits her. *Ethan Goon, Theo Goon, Dylan Super-Goon, and Eli Dumber-than-Dumb Goon.* The names run through her mind like a litany, each one tied to a specific, unpleasant memory. But it's the fifth figure that catches her attention—a face she doesn't know, a man who is still eerily calm, almost detached from the growing tension around him.

Who the hell is he? The thought lingers, even as she braces herself for whatever is about to come.

"What the fuck are you doing, not only in my territory

but in my parking lot?" Charlotte demands, her voice laced with a spike of Alpha energy. She knows it won't command them, but it serves as a reminder of the power she keeps carefully hidden beneath the surface.

Ethan steps forward, a sarcastic smirk on his face. "Miles sends his love," blowing her a mocking kiss, "and a message." he sneers.

Charlotte's eyes narrow, her lips curling into a dangerous smile. "What does the King of mange poodles want me to know?" she retorts, watching with satisfaction as the insult lands, making the goons bristle with anger.

The newcomer, however, remains unfazed, his expression unreadable. *Interesting,* she notes.

"Miles says he'll give you North Las Vegas and Henderson," Ethan spits out, the words dripping with contempt.

Charlotte can't believe what she just heard, but she keeps her face impassive. They don't deserve the satisfaction of seeing her react. Stretching the silence, making Ethan visibly uncomfortable.

He fidgets under her steady gaze, finally blurting out, "Well, should I tell him you accept the terms?"

A slow burn of anger ignites in Charlotte's veins, but she stays still, letting the tension build. She watches every twitch, every bead of sweat forming on their foreheads, relishing the discomfort her silence causes. She hopes they'll use what little intelligence they have, turn around, and take her answer back to their idiot of an Alpha.

But... they don't. One second, she's standing there, holding her ground, and the next, her wolf takes over in a blur of motion. Her claws slash across one wolf's neck as she shifts mid-leap, landing on all fours with a feral growl.

The four wolves rush at her from all directions, a blur of fur and fangs, but Charlotte is faster. She's smaller, yes, but her speed and experience are her weapons, honed by countless battles.

She moves like a shadow, dodging claws and teeth with lethal precision. Her wolf is in its element, reveling in the chaos, the thrill of the fight.

Eli lunges at her, his jaws snapping inches from her throat, but Charlotte is quicker.

She spins on her hind legs, her powerful muscles propelling her forward, and her teeth sink deep into his back leg.

The satisfying crunch of bone is followed by Eli's sharp yelp, a sound that fuels the fire burning in her chest. The taste of his blood on her tongue only heightens her bloodlust, and she shakes her head violently, tearing at the flesh before releasing him with a snarl.

But there's no time to celebrate. Dylan's light brown wolf barrels into her from the side, his fangs ripping into the side of her neck. Pain flares white-hot as his teeth tear through muscle and sinew, and she feels the warm rush of blood trickling down her fur, soaking into the earth below. The wound stings, but it's a distant concern-her mind is a battlefield of strategy, not a place for weakness.

To an observer, it might seem like chaos, a whirlwind of fur and blood, but to Charlotte, it's a calculated dance of death and survival. She tracks each enemy with razor-sharp focus, using her training to anticipate their moves, staying one step ahead of the pack.

Her claws rake across Dylan's flank, ripping through skin and muscle, the coppery scent of blood thick in the air. The taste of war fills her mouth, and her wolf drinks it in, reveling in the violence.

The air is filled with the sounds of battle-snarls, yelps, the sickening thud of bodies colliding. Charlotte's heart pounds in her chest, but her mind stays clear, calculating. She twists and turns, her claws finding purchase in fur and flesh, her jaws snapping at any wolf that dares to come too close.

Blood spatters the ground, a crimson reminder of the stakes at play, but she doesn't let it distract her. She's in control, and she's ready to spill every drop of blood necessary to protect what's hers.

But as she fights, she notices the unfamiliar grey wolf isn't attacking with the same ferocity. He swats at her with human-like speed, far slower than he should be.

Charlotte dodges easily, catching his front leg with her claws, but choosing not to inflict any real damage.

Something about him feels different–off–but she doesn't have time to analyze him now.

Despite her strength, the four goons finally start acting like wolves, using coordinated attacks to wear her down.

Ethan pins her to the ground, and she struggles to break free as Dylan's wolf charges toward her throat.

This is going to hurt, she thinks, bracing herself.

But just as Dylan is about to strike, a black streak barrels into him from the side, knocking him off course.

In a split second, Charlotte realizes none of the goons are black.

The sudden appearance of another wolf throws Ethan off balance just enough for her to shove him away.

Scrambling to her paws, she watches the mammoth, obsidian black wolf tear into Dylan's throat with savage precision.

Her wolf is hyper-aware of him, watching with something akin to admiration as he shreds Dylan's neck, the life leaving his eyes in a slow, gruesome process.

The air is filled with the sickening sounds of bones

popping and cracking as Dylan shifts back to his human form, lifeless on the ground.

Eli yowls in pain, "Bitch! Look at my fucking leg!"

Charlotte's wolf fights against the shift, but with a growl of frustration, she forces the transformation. Her bones crack and realign, fur receding as her human form takes over.

Pushing herself up from her crouched position, her muscles trembling from the effort, blood seeping from the deep claw marks in her neck and thigh. Her breath comes in ragged gasps, but she forces herself to stand tall, her eyes narrowing as they lock onto Ethan, a silent promise of vengeance burning in her gaze.

His voice wavers as he speaks, "I'll let Miles know your answer. Be prepared, she-wolf. The Cascade Pack *will* take this territory. No matter who you bring to help." Shooting a venomous glare at the massive black wolf, who now stands protectively in front of Charlotte, fangs bared and ready for more.=

Standing over the lifeless body, the lone wolf's chest heaves as he struggles to catch his breath. Adrenaline still buzzing with a deep sense of pride swelling within him.

She's mine, the wolf growls possessively, irritated that the she-wolf had shifted back to human. Instinct had driven him to protect her, and instinct was never wrong.

With considerable effort, Liam wrestles back control, forcing his wolf to retreat as his human form takes shape.

He's instantly aware of two things: first, he's very naked; second, he's standing in front of the most breathtaking woman he's ever seen. The cool breeze teases his skin, reminding him of his current state of nakedness. His hands shoot down, covering himself as best as he can.

The woman is also completely naked, but she's radiating a confidence that only makes her more irresistible. The way her eyes trail over him, unapologetically taking in every inch, sends a jolt of awareness straight to his groin.

Don't pop a boner. Don't pop a boner, he silently pleads, willing his body to behave.

"Umm, hi," he stammers, his voice betraying the nerves coursing through him. "I need to run back to my truck and grab some clothes. Will you stay here?" He forgets himself for a split second, gesturing behind him, his hand dropping just long enough to expose himself again. "Oh shit!" he curses, quickly covering up, his face flushing with embarrassment. "That way I can properly introduce myself?"

The goddess before him–with her long jet-black hair and piercing green eyes–slowly acknowledges his request, her gaze never wavering.

"I'll be right over there. That's my truck. I need to grab some clothes, too," she replies, her voice calm, though her eyes continue to bore into him with an intensity he can't quite decipher. *Is she angry that I saved her?* he wonders, unease creeping in.

Liam nods, then turns on his heel and jogs toward his truck, his hands still awkwardly covering himself. The jog turns into more of a waddle, and he can feel his face burning as he mutters under his breath, "What the fuck? What the fuck did you just do, Wolf?" Inside, he feels his wolf's satisfaction, almost like he's... smiling. *Smiling! Seriously?* "You stupid S.O.B."

Liam and his wolf have always been complete opposites–Wolf is pure instinct, a creature of raw power and primal urges, while Liam is driven by emotion, sometimes to a fault. And right now, the swirling confusion of emotions–embarrassment, attraction, bewilderment–is messing with his head. The full gamut of feelings surging through him is making it hard to think straight, and he's never felt more out of his depth.

He is a lone wolf just trying to hide out in the city for a few days, but now? Now he has a kill on his hands and there will be some pack hunting him for payback.

Dammit Wolf! What did you do? He can feel Wolf's still puffy chest.

When those assholes shifted and went after that female, all logic disappeared from his vision, and as much as Liam doesn't want to admit it, it wasn't just Wolf that wanted blood. He saw red, and that red was the blood he was going to spill for even daring to touch her.

Her wolf was the most beautiful creature he had ever seen. Black as a new moon night, with a single grey sock marking her left leg and paw, she was striking. He hadn't intervened to play the hero; he attacked because instinct had driven him to protect. And once again, the question nagged at him: *What the fuck?*

Opening the back window of his older Ford Bronco, Liam's fingers brush against the familiar rust spot just to his right. His ol' girl has a few rough patches, but he doesn't see them as flaws—more like badges of honor, marking the years they've taken care of each other. He bought her in his twenties, and she's been his steadfast companion ever since.

He digs into his *"Oops, I shifted too soon"* tote, rummaging for clothes. His hand closes around a pair of black workout pants, and as he is trying to put them on, his toe catches on the elastic band, nearly sending him face-first into the pavement.

"Fuck," he mutters, steadying himself. His favorite hoodie is right on top–a black sweatshirt that has miraculously stayed intact all these years. Charmed by the cat on the front holding a pick and trowel, with a speech bubble that proudly declares, *"Geology Rocks!"*

He throws it over his head, then adjusts the black-rimmed glasses on his nose, a small smile tugging at his lips.

As he scans the parking lot, trying to remember exactly where the stunning she-wolf pointed, he realizes he was too distracted by covering his love nuggets to notice. But then, the sun glints off her shiny hair, and he spots her by a jacked-up Ram pickup. *Impressive,* he thinks, feeling a surge of admiration.

His smile widens as the delectable scent from the gym fills his senses once again. He hadn't planned on using that gym more than once, but that scent had his wolf craving more. He's been coming back, searching for the source. And now, that source has his entire body on high alert.

Jogging over to where she stands—sadly, now fully clothed–he holds out his hand. "Hi, my name is Liam Dunne."

"Hey, I'm Charlotte." Her voice is cool, measured, but there's a fire behind it. "What the fuck did you do, Liam Dunne? You came out of nowhere. I'm no damsel in distress. You just injected yourself into a war you know nothing about."

Liam blinks, taken aback by her intensity. But he quickly recovers, his own voice laced with sarcasm. "Yeah, sure, you're welcome for saving your throat. I saw you holding your own, but when that wolf was about to go for the kill while another pinned you down? Nah. No way, my wolf wasn't having any of that bullshit. That's not fair game and shows no honor. I couldn't just stand there and let it happen."

Her gaze softens slightly, though only a fraction. "Thanks for leveling the odds," she says, her head held high. Liam can see it—this is a woman who knows how to take care of herself, who doesn't need saving. But that small, grudging thank you makes both Wolf and the man stand a little taller. It's a confusing sensation, one he's not used to, but it makes him feel... good.

Movement catches Liam's eye, and he glances over to see the wolf without a throat being unceremoniously tossed into the back of a black, windowless Mercedes van by a striking woman with smooth, rich umber-colored skin. She's beautiful, no doubt, but she doesn't hold a candle to the raven-haired vixen standing in front of him.

When he looks back at Charlotte, she's giving a brief wave of thanks. The look on his face must've betrayed his thoughts.

"That's Jade," she explains, her voice even. Turning back to him, "She's our pack cleaner. We're no strangers to being attacked unexpectedly."

Liam nods in understanding, "Thank you for taking care of it."

"Well, Liam Dunne, I have to get going. Thanks again for not letting those dickweeds give me a hickey that would never go away." She turns, her hand reaching for the truck door.

"Wait!" The word bursts out of him before he can stop it. "Is this a good gym, Charlotte?"

She pauses, turning back to him, a teasing smile curling her lips. "This?" She points at the large wolf lifting barbells on the side of the grey building. "This is the best gym in Las Vegas, but I'm biased."

"Why is that?" Liam's whole body tingles when that sexy smile of hers slowly takes over her face.

"I own it." She climbs into her truck with an easy grace, giving him a wave through the window as she starts the engine.

Fuuuuuuck. Liam stands there, rooted to the spot as the truck pulls away, his mind a whirlwind of emotions. All these feelings, confusing the hell out of him, leave him reeling. He hasn't felt this way since... since Sophie.

Charlotte mutters to herself, "Holy shit! What in the actual fuck just happened?" Her eyes glued to the rearview mirror as she watches the six foot five hunk stride back to his truck. *Unfortunately clothed,* she thinks, biting her lip.

His thighs, thick like tree trunks, look like they were carved from stone, and they needed to be—to hold up those perfectly chiseled abs and that massive chest she can't stop daydreaming about running her hands all over.

He took down Dylan with alarming speed, his wolf twice the size of hers, radiating pure, unfiltered power. She could practically taste the Alpha energy rolling off him, but his human side? That didn't act like an Alpha at all. With that ridiculous hoodie, he gave off more of a Clark Kent nerd vibe. And those glasses?

Shifters don't need glasses, she muses, but then her thoughts take a turn. *He can definitely keep them on—and nothing else—while I rub every inch of that chest.*

Her wolf is restless, growling and nipping at her consciousness, pissed that Charlotte let him leave. One might think she'd be more concerned about the battle that just took place, but her wolf's singular focus is on one thing: *It was him. That scent was him.*

That scent—smokey and charged with adrenaline— wraps around her senses, making her pulse race.

Fucking hell, she curses inwardly. She does not need this shit right now. His scent is doing things to her, making her want to act on instincts she's kept buried. She's been so focused on getting her pack into one place, holding their territory, that she's neglected other... needs. That has to be it.

But that man... just the memory of him makes her skin tingle in a way she's never felt. And what the hell is up with her nipples? They're so sensitive now that her bra feels like sandpaper.

Damn it, she thinks, shaking her head in disbelief. *I better give Jason a call.* It's time to take care of this little problem before it spirals out of control.

THE DICKSHROOM MASTERPIECE

C harlotte paces around the game room, her footsteps soft against the polished floor as she recounts the attack in the parking lot. "That pecker nose, Ethan, had me pinned while Dylan was within inches of ripping out my throat," she says, her voice laced with frustration. "But then, out of nowhere, this massive black wolf charges in?"

Jade straightens from her shot, eyes narrowing as if silently urging Charlotte to spill more details.

Harper, leaning casually against the table, mirroring Jade's unspoken question with a raised eyebrow, her gaze now focused intently on Charlotte.

Across the room, Luna sits crisscross apple sauce on the floor, completely engrossed in her paint-by-numbers project —a picture of dicks cleverly disguised as mushrooms.

The scene is so quintessentially Luna that Charlotte can already picture this absurd masterpiece framed and hanging somewhere in the house, a perfect testament to Luna's offbeat sense of humor.

Jade takes her shot, the crack of the cue ball echoing

through the room. "So, I say we head up to Shasta and just kill the bastards in their sleep." Her tone is casual, as if she's suggesting a weekend getaway rather than a bloodbath.

Charlotte knows Jade is the type who prefers action over deliberation, the kind of person who believes in eliminating threats before they become problems. *Kill first, ask questions later,* that's Jade's motto.

Harper, ever the voice of reason, shakes her head as she leans over the table, lining up her shot. "Jade, you know we can't do that. With the constant battles between our packs, everyone would know it was us. And if we suddenly wipe out the Cascade Pack, their allies will have all eyes on us and our lands."

Charlotte sighs, watching Harper sink the 9-ball with a smooth stroke. She's right. Hell, they're both right.

I would love nothing more than to end the Cascade Pack and be done with it, but we can't risk drawing more enemies out of the woodwork.

She paces in front of the large picture window that over-looks the metallic pool, the shimmering lights of the Vegas Strip twinkling in the distance. The house is a strange mix of elegance and gothic style–white walls, black accents, and random splashes of color that hint at a darker aesthetic. She often wonders who built it. *Maybe I'll ask Willamena if it was one of her coven members.*

"We don't want to open a can of balls we can't juggle," Charlotte says, turning away from the window. "But I think we may have to call a challenge."

Luna's paintbrush stills in her hand, her eyes wide and glistening with unshed tears. "But if we do, we could lose everything!" she exclaims, her voice trembling. "I love this house, and I love Vegas. I don't want to leave here."

Charlotte pauses, her gaze drifting back to the city

skyline. The sight of it always brings a mix of emotions—this city saved them when they needed it most, offering sanctuary when nowhere else could. And now, it's up to them to protect it. *But twats like the Cascade Pack wouldn't understand that; they'd ruin it without a second thought.*

"Okay, let's sleep on it tonight," Charlotte finally says, turning back to the others. "If you come up with any other ideas, I'm all ears." She knows she's been holding back, not mentioning the stranger, Liam Dunne. She told them how he took down Dylan, how they exchanged a few words, and how he left. But she wonders if Jade caught on to her omission. If she did, Jade doesn't say anything, her focus is back on the game.

Jade hits the freshly racked balls with force, the crack reverberating through the room. "Have the COPS called yet?" she asks, watching the scattering balls.

In their world—the world of shifters and other non-human beings–COPS means something entirely different: the Council of the Paranormal Society. The agency was created about five years ago, after a human accidentally caught a wolf shifting in broad daylight.

There were too many witnesses and video's to pass it off this time, and the revelation had thrown the paranormal world into chaos.

"No," Charlotte replies, shaking her head. "I don't think any humans saw, but as we know, those wily little fuckers keep that shit quiet until it suits them."

The human government had been well aware of the potential fallout–mass chaos and panic on both sides. Paranormals feared capture and experimentation, while humans became terrified that their worst nightmares were suddenly all too real.

Luna's eyes widen with concern. "You shifted to protect yourself, so they can't come after you, right?"

Charlotte exhales, considering the implications. "I guess it depends on whether there's a video and what it shows of the fight. We filed a complaint with Jase, so the council knows the Cascades have been a problem for us." She barely finishes her sentence when her phone rings, the timing uncanny. Her eyes widen as she looks up at the others, then answers with a smirk, "Were your ears burning, Jase?"

"Oh, so you do talk about me?" Jase's voice comes through, laced with a teasing tone.

"Yeah, but it's nothing good. We were just saying Jase is a pencil dick who needs to get a real truck." Charlotte can't help but smile. Their banter is as familiar as it is playful. She can practically hear Jase rolling his eyes on the other end, knowing how much he loves his gun-metal grey Ford.

"At least my Raptor doesn't look like it was painted at the nail salon."

Ignoring his attempt at wit, Charlotte rolls her eyes and cuts straight to the point. "What the fuck do you want, Jase?"

"Can dish but not take. What do you know about a lone wolf coming through Vegas? It's your territory, so I know you know something. You ladies don't fuck around, so what's up with him being there?"

"I don't know much. He was at my gym so we exchanged pleasantries. His name is Liam Dunne." She gives up the name only because Jase already knows. He would use it to see if she would lie.

"That's it? Did you send him packing?"

"Pretty much. I told him not to stay too long." Charlotte tries to keep her voice blasé.

"That's it? You? You told him not to stay too long?" Jase has always been a skeptical one.

"Yeah. He seemed like a nice guy. He wanted to see the sites. It's not a big deal, Jase. He's not here starting shit with my pack, killing them and trying to take my territory." Charlotte puts some extra energy behind this little rant.

"Woah Nelly. Ok. Ok. I just thought I would check in. Let me know if he becomes a problem."

"Why? Unless a human is involved, you can't do anything," she throws some snark into that, "so I guess I'll call if he gets too close to a human." Charlotte makes sure her disgust for C.O.P.S laws comes through.

"Ok, Charlotte. I hear you. I know the laws piss you off. You got my number if the Cascades step out of line even a centimeter with a 'human around' call me." And the line goes dead.

Charlotte puts her phone in her back pocket. "Apparently, he didn't want to flirt anymore. Well, you heard all that. Do you think he knows about the fight in the parking lot?"

"Of course he does. How else would he know there was a lone wolf here?" Jade is standing against the wall with pool stick in hand. "No humans must've saw or he wouldn't have called. He would be pounding down the door."

Charlotte nods her head. "Agreed." Jade is right. Jase knows more than he is letting on.

LAVENDER AND ORANGES

L ying on the too-firm bed of a dated hotel just off the strip, Liam scans the room. It's clean, but not enough to distract him from its half-hearted makeover.

The old wood paneling, now painted white, reveals its age with brown seeping through in patches. The faux wood laminate under his feet pops with every step, reminding him this place is no luxury stay. Not that he cares-he doesn't plan to be here long enough to worry about the bed's lack of comfort. But as he stares at the ceiling, his mind is consumed by *her*.

That scent. God, it's stuck in his head. Lavender and oranges, sweet and sharp. Now, even the faintest whiff of citrus has him hard.

He shifts, trying to ease the strain, but the pressure only makes it worse. His hand drifts below his waistband, slipping beneath the elastic. The relief is instant, but it's not enough. He grips his cock, tight, and begins to stroke, his mind replaying those bright green eyes-piercing through his thoughts as his hand moves, slow at first, then faster. Every pump sends him spiraling deeper into the fantasy.

His breath hitches as images of her fill his mind: her sun-kissed skin, soft and golden, straddling his hips. His left hand works its way lower, cupping his balls as his right hand speeds up. Her breasts, perfectly round, begging to be touched, to be tasted. He can almost feel her lips on his, her scent wrapping around him, driving him insane.

Up, down, up, down. His stomach tightens, heat building as he pictures her body pressed against his. His hand moves faster now, a desperate rhythm, and with a final stroke, he grits his teeth. The first stream of warmth hits his hand, and her name slips from his lips in a hoarse whisper. "Charlotte…"

Relief floods him, unexpected but needed. Ever since he caught that intoxicating scent in the gym, he's been wound tighter than leggings on a horse. He wanted to ask for her number, but deep down he knew better. If he had it, there'd be no stopping him.

He knows he should leave, pack up his shit, get in the Bronco, and head east. Getting his dick wet wasn't part of the plan. But after that release, he realizes it wouldn't be enough. Not with her.

He needs to leave. Now. If he's smart, he'll get the hell out of here. But then again… he's never pretended to be smart.

IT'S A TRAP

Charlotte sinks into the ten-person in-ground spa, settling in front of her favorite jets. The warm water pulses against her back as her thoughts drift to her time with the Black Canyon Pack.

"That was better, but you can shift faster. Do it again. Help your wolf understand that these shifts will save both of your lives. She needs to let you take control when shifting. Now. Do it again."

Lifting the can of seltzer to her lips, Charlotte lets the bubbles pop on her tongue as betraying thoughts drift to him—six-five and impossible to ignore. A brown-haired, brown-eyed mountain of a man, all muscle and olive skin.

That ass... She can't stop picturing it, the cute way he waddled away from her. *Cute?* What the hell is wrong with her? *Liam Dunne. Where the hell did you come from, and why are you in Vegas?*

Could his arrival and the Cascade Pack's return be connected?

Her wolf gives a low growl at the thought. *Fine,* she scolds. *He's not here to hurt us. Stop growling.*

Still, the questions won't leave her alone. What's he doing in Vegas? His plates were from California. Is he mated? He didn't smell mated. The thoughts nags at her, but she shakes it off.

"Get your shit together, Charlotte. He's just a lone wolf passing through," she mutters under her breath, glancing around to make sure none of the other ladies heard. The last thing she needs is to look like some love-sick middle schooler. *You're an Alpha fucking Female, for Christ's sake. Tighten the bra straps and focus on saving your pack and your lands.*

A sharp ring slices through her thoughts, and *Potential Spam* flashes across her phone screen. With a sigh, Charlotte sets the phone down, resisting the urge to silence it altogether. Right now, she just wants to sink deeper into her own thoughts, undisturbed.

Two seconds later, it dings again. She glances down and rolls her eyes at the text from an unknown number:

Answer your phone. It'll be worth your time.

When the phone rings again, she answers, but there's no time for pleasantries.

"If you want to save your pack, meet me at the fountains. I'll find you-and only you. Be there at ten tonight."

Charlotte's jaw tightens. "How do I know this isn't a trap to get me away from my pack?" Her voice drips with aggression.

"If I wanted to attack, I wouldn't pick the most human conjested place in Vegas. Plus, I hate the Cascade Pack as much as you do, and the way I see it, the enemy of my enemy is my friend."

The line goes dead.

Well, fuck. Looks like she's about to take the second biggest risk of her life at ten.

LONE WOLF

Liam knows he should leave, but who comes to Vegas and skips the Strip? He can't just blow through town without seeing the Eiffel Tower or Caesar's Palace. Or without catching another glimpse of that stunning gym owner who's got his thoughts all twisted.

Deep down, he knows it's just an excuse to stick around, but hell, that's not something he's about to admit to himself. What are the chances of running into her again, anyway?

There are thousands of tourists milling around, weighed down by shopping bags and clutching oversized slushy drinks.

Liam walks down Vegas Boulevard, slipping one earbud into his ear, then the other. With a quick tap, the world around him muffles—voices, music, and the chaotic honking of cars fade as the noise cancellation kicks in with a satisfying *tunk*. He draws in a deep breath, feeling the weight of the Strip's immensity pressing in from all sides. The neon lights flash above him, but the constant roar of the city is starting to wear thin.

Fingers brushing his pocket, he pulls out his phone,

ready to turn on his favorite playlist. His thumb freezes over the screen. *Another missed call.* Brian. His old Alpha.

The ache creeps in, familiar and unwanted. It's been two years since his mate died, and despite countless attempts to adjust to pack life without her, it never felt right. Nothing was the same.

Six months, seven days and nineteen hours ago, Liam decided he needed a break, so he packed up and traveled east. The original plan was to travel for a month, maybe two, but it seems fate has other plans.

He hung out in Idaho for a while but a she-wolf caused him a bit of trouble so he moved on.

Wyoming was nice, but the assholes that hate wolves also carry big guns.

When he accepted the lone wolf status, he knew he would be a nomad forever. From Wyoming, he turned south and landed in Las Vegas. It was only supposed to be for a week, but then came that scent.

This woman has him discombobulated. These feelings of protectiveness, lust, and unfounded trust, reminds him of how he felt with Sophie.

He's heard of pairings after a mate has passed, but those are more for companionship. Wolves are rooted in connections and are extremely social, so having a partner becomes more of an agreement than deep-seated love. A second love mate isn't unheard of, but it's rare.

He rubs the top of his head, a nervous habit he's never managed to shake. Fate allows exceptions, but it's rare to find more than one true mate. Sophie was his. A submissive, gentle soul, she endured the cruelty of pack bullies in their youth, and Liam's protectiveness was forged early. They became high school sweethearts, mating shortly after he returned from college in Portland.

Losing her had shattered something vital in him—and in his wolf.

But being near Charlotte... it's different. It feels good. Comfortable in a way he hasn't felt in years. And strong, as if she's the piece that could finally balance the chaos he's been carrying since Sophie's death.

His wolf starts tearing at his insides and it jars him out of his musings. The beast within, hates humans on a good day, so to be surrounded by their patchouli and skunk weed... nope, he needs to find a clearing in the chaos.

His wolf is still pissed but that's fairly normal, so Liam gives a shrug. He looks down at his phone again while making his way to the coffee shop. Is he really ready to have this conversation? When the past isn't said out loud, it's easy to ignore. He lost his light on November eleventh, two years ago and talking about it makes it real.

He orders his coffee, then finds a seat in the corner. Flipping his phone over in his large palm, he takes a deep breath before hitting send. He doesn't want to chicken out again. It rings once before Brian's deep voice greets him. "Liam, Brother. Thank you for calling back."

Liam can't find the words, so he sits there looking at the ground.

"Ok, Brother. I understand, just listen. The pack wants you to know... Hell, I want you to know we are sorry, man. We are so very sorry we weren't more aware of the hell you were going through when Sophie died. We thought we were doing what was best for you by getting you back out into the pack. Getting you back to work. None of us realized it would be torture to see all the other couples. We support the break from the pack but want you to know home is here anytime you are ready. We are here and we'll work on having a better understanding so we can support you."

Brian's words hit him. This is not what he expected. Liam digs for his strength.

"Brian, the pack did nothing wrong. None of us knew how to handle Sophie's death. Not even me." Liam drags a hand across the back of his neck, gaze lowering briefly. "The pack was grieving too. We all did the best we could."

He exhales slowly.

"My leaving wasn't about the pack. I just... couldn't heal surrounded by memories of her everywhere I looked. Thank you for offering to let me come home."

The next breath fills deeper, heavier.

"I felt the pack bond leave me about three months ago." The words come quieter now, rough around the edges. "I've accepted that I'm a lone wolf."

Silence stretches a beat before he forces himself to continue.

"Tell the pack thank you. For trying to keep me steady through the worst days of my life." His jaw tightens once. "You're a good Alpha, Brian. Keep them safe. Keep them happy."

A half a minute of their breathing, processing the love and respect they have for one another goes by. Brian is the one to break the silence, "We will always have your back, Liam. You call if you need anything at all." And the line goes dead.

THE ENEMY OF MY ENEMY
IS STILL MY ENEMY?

After the call from her new frenemy, Charlotte knew she needed to get out of the house. The ladies would be suspicious if she left at nine o'clock at night.

Luna would probably start questioning, "Who is he? Will I like him? Does he have a big schlong?"

And Jade would get dressed for war because... well, it's dark outside and Charlotte may need backup.

Charlotte briefly considers making that call to Jason. She saw a post about him being back in Vegas—maybe a quick booty call at his place would kill some time. But the thought sits wrong, unsettling in a way she can't quite shake. Her wolf isn't having it either, grumbling inside her, making her pay for even thinking about it.

"Why are you so damn cranky?" she mutters under her breath, feeling the tension coil tighter. "I'll make time tomorrow for a run. Stop being such a bitch."

After debating every option she has no energy for, Charlotte finally settles on the gym. Hitting something feels safer than saying something, and maybe if she pushes her body hard enough, her brain will shut up for a minute.

Shortly after sneaking into the garage—quiet as she can be, keys barely jingling—Charlotte fires up the truck and pulls out before anyone can stop her. She knows they heard it. Of course they did. The whole damn house has supernatural hearing and a sixth sense for when she's avoiding her feelings.

She's barely halfway down the driveway when her phone lights up on the console.

She lets out a humorless laugh, shaking her head.

Yeah. They definitely heard the truck.

> Where are you going Alpha? Need back-up?

No. I just have to run to the gym for a minute. I'll be home before dark.

> But it's already dark.

Oops, Hadn't noticed 😅

Throwing the phone in the passenger seat, she doesn't even bother turning the music on.

Silence settles around her like a heavy coat, the kind that traps more heat than it comforts. The hum of the engine, the tires rolling over asphalt—normally those sounds anchor her. Tonight, they just give her too much space to think.

Her fingers tighten around the steering wheel.

This is the part she hates about driving. The autopilot. The stillness. One open road and her mind slips sideways, falling into places she keeps barricaded behind steel doors.

Present. Future. Past. They all blur when she's alone like this.

A breath slips out of her, too sharp.

And that's when it hits her.

Harper's whisper—soft, shaking—ghosts through her ear so vividly she has to blink hard to stay grounded.

"I'm scared, Char."

The memory grabs her by the spine and drags her backward.

Suddenly the air in the SUV feels colder, thinner, like she's breathing that night again instead of now.

She's not driving.

She's crawling.

Mud squishes between her fingers—cold, heavy, clinging to her skin the way dread clung to her bones. Her heart is pounding so loud she remembers thinking the Enforcers would hear it. Behind her, Harper and Jade move in near-silent terror, their shallow breaths barely audible over the rustling leaves.

She can still taste the fear.

Metallic. Sharp. Shared.

Their bond had been humming that night, so tight it was hard to tell whose panic belonged to who. Harper's terror wrapped around Charlotte's chest like a fist, squeezing with every breath.

She remembers every detail.

The field ahead of them, an endless black sea under a moonless sky. The wet grass brushing her arms. The darkness so thick it swallowed everything except the three of them.

And thank the gods for the powder. Not because Charlotte had found it. But because her mother had.

They already had the escape planned. Every route. Every signal. Every minute accounted for. This was supposed to be their shot.

But Charlotte still felt like something was missing.

She slipped into her father's office after dark, hands shaking as she pulled open drawers she should've never dared to touch.

She wasn't acting on impulse—she was hunting. Searching for anything that could give them an edge. A distraction. A weapon. A miracle. She didn't know what she was looking for, only that the plan felt incomplete without... something she couldn't name.

Something to tip the scales.

She hadn't even gotten the drawers fully open when her mother appeared in the doorway. Not storming. Not screaming.

Just... standing there.

Frozen. Like she'd walked in on a crime she'd been waiting her whole life to witness.

Charlotte remembers staring back, heart hammering, already bracing for the punishment.

Even now, what floors Charlotte most about that night is what her mother *didn't* do. She didn't shout for her father. She didn't march over and wrench Charlotte to her knees. She didn't react the way she always had when Charlotte stepped out of line.

She just... stopped. And looked at her, like a woman waking up.

Then... she stepped into the room, closed the door with a soft click and walked past Charlotte without a word.

Straight to the bottom drawer. There below some papers, she pulled out a rusty tin holding a small jar of white powder.

Her mother's hands shook as she held it. Fear strumming through the small bit of bond they had left.

She pressed the tin into Charlotte's palms and whispered, barely audible: *"Don't breathe it in."*

A pause.

A tremble.

Then—

"When you put it in his coffee."

Charlotte had been too young, too terrified to understand the layers in that moment. But now? Now she knows exactly what her mother meant.

She was giving Charlotte the means to kill him. Or protect herself. Or escape. Maybe all three.

It was the one and only time her mother ever chose her.

Charlotte remembers her fingers trembling so hard she nearly dropped the tin. Remembers the way her mother's eyes darted to the door, terrified he would appear. Remembers the unspoken plea in her voice.

Run. Fight. Do what I never could.

She didn't know exactly what the powder would do—only that her father hid it, only that her mother feared it, only that using it was her only chance.

And when she mixed it into the Enforcers' coffee later that night—smiling sweetly, hands shaking—Charlotte realizes now she wasn't just fueled by fear.

She was fueled by her mother's single, final act of defiance.

And it worked. They'd dropped. And she'd run, dragging the girls with her.

No time for second thoughts.

Freedom was close that night—close enough to taste. And yet every inch forward had felt like a mile. Every rustle sounded like a hand grabbing for their ankles. Every breath felt too loud.

She remembers Harper whispering to keep herself from breaking.

"We're almost out. We're almost free. Right, Char?"

And she remembers lying, because Harper needed hope more than Charlotte needed the truth.

Jade had been quiet, nerves wound tight, voice low as she questioned the sanctuary waiting for them over the ridge. And Charlotte had given the only answer she had—that they had to trust someone, sometime, or die where they stood.

The moment they made it over that ridge, Charlotte wanted to cry. Wanted to scream at the top of her lungs. *"Fuck You!"* But she didn't.

Once again Harper's whispers bring her to the exact moment.

"Holy shit. We did it."

Dropping into the trees. The relief of shedding their packs. The burn of cold water sliding down her throat. The ache in her muscles that told her she was still alive.

And then the shifts.

Jade first—bones reshaping in slow, controlled agony.

Harper brushing her fingers through thick fur like it kept her steady.

And then Charlotte, stripping off wet clothes, letting her wolf slam forward with a fury that had been building for years.

Her paws hitting the earth.

The ground trembling beneath her weight.

Harper taking a step back on instinct.

Charlotte remembers all of it—the fear, the pain, the

jokes Harper cracked just to keep them breathing. But most of all, she remembers the moment the three of them ran.

Three girls.

Three wolves.

Three hearts breaking and healing at the same time.

Freedom wasn't a place.

It started that night—in the mud, in the dark, in the breathless whisper of a girl who trusted her.

Charlotte's grip tightens on the steering wheel as the memory fades, leaving her chest pulled tight and her pulse uneven.

Charlotte pulls into the parking lot, her headlights sweeping across a chaotic scene. Paparazzi swarm the front entrance like vultures, their bodies jostling for position, lenses gleaming as they zero in on their prey. Confusion flickers across her face, she hadn't heard anything about a celebrity visit. She glances toward the quieter back of the building, debating her options before steering toward the side door.

She slips inside, the muffled buzz of the gym filtering through the hallway. The familiar hum settles her nerves as she makes her way to her office, glancing through the large window that frames the main floor. Just a regular Tuesday night—nothing out of the ordinary, or so it seems. She strolls to the guest service counter, where Pat is folding towels, the snap of fabric breaking through the steady hum

"Hey, Charlotte," Pat greets her, glancing up. "What brings you back?"

"I just wanted to burn off some energy," Charlotte says, her eyes drifting toward the front door, brows knitting in confusion. "But what's going on outside?"

Pat brushes the air. "oh, that? That's a bunch of fools that don't know how to fact-check before they turn into vultures trying to get their money shot."

Charlotte shakes her head, signaling she needs more information.

"Someone posted that Dirk Kane was working out here." Pat shouts toward the doors, dragging out the words. "Of course, he's nooooooot, you tramps. He posted from his verified account that he's in Spain right now." Without missing a beat, he switches back to his normal tone, eyes on the towels he's folding. "Fucking morons."

Charlotte bites back a laugh but quickly gives in, a grin tugging at the corners of her lips. "So, no high-profile clients that need backup?"

Pat shakes his head, a smirk tugging at his lips. "Nah, not unless you count this fabulous haircut I just got as high-profile." He flicks his wrist dramatically, as if brushing long hair over his shoulder. "We're just sneaking everyone out through the emergency exit so they don't have to deal with those assholes."

"Perfect. Thanks for handling it," Charlotte says with a nod, a small smile tugging at her lips. She pauses, glancing at Pat with mock seriousness. "And Pat... the hair is *most definitely* high-profile. Might even need its own security detail."

Still needing to burn off energy—but not in the mood to deal with clients or the chaos outside—she retreats to her office. The quiet haven houses her private rowing machine, the perfect outlet to work off the restlessness gnawing at her.

Each pull of the handle tightens her muscles, the rhythm steady and grounding. The machine glides smoothly beneath her, the motion soothing in its repetition. Time blurs as the tension in her body begins to ease, though her mind stays fixed on the secret meeting ahead.

This better be worth it. The thought nags at her, sharp and bitter. Killing someone on the Strip wasn't exactly on today's To-Do list, but if it came to that, she'd make it work.

Charlotte weaves through the crowd, dodging strollers, fanny packs, and bright red "I Love Vegas" t-shirts. Her mind races with questions, each one tumbling over the next. *Who is this asshole? Why here? Why ten o'clock? Is he trying to get the council involved?*

The memory of the gym parking lot flashes in her mind. She got lucky then—no humans saw the scene. But here? On the Strip? With all these cameras and tourists? There's no way she could shift without turning into a media frenzy.

Reaching the fountains, she positions herself with her back to the water. Around her, the crowd buzzes with anticipation, all eyes waiting for the show to begin. Meanwhile, her senses stay sharp, scanning the sea of faces for whoever is about to make this night even more complicated.

With a sharp crack, the fountains burst to life, water leaping and twisting in sync with the opening chords of *Viva Las Vegas*. The crowd erupts into gasps and cheers, but Charlotte doesn't blink. She knows better than to be distracted by the spectacle. One slip of focus could turn this night into chaos.

Her head stays on a swivel, eyes scanning every face, every movement. The crowd feels thicker, louder, but her senses cut through the noise, hunting for anything off. And then... there. A familiar face pushes through the layers of tourists. He stops, just far enough back, hovering behind a wall of bodies. Their eyes meet, locking across the distance. Charlotte doesn't flinch. Doesn't move. She refuses to give up the upper hand, not in such a public place.

What the hell is he playing at? Her mind spins as the fountains behind her rise and fall to the beat of Elvis, splashing light over the crowd. The oohs and aahs wash over her, but her gaze stays glued to him-the stranger who's been lurking in the shadows, the one who hasn't made a single move.

Their stare holds, unbroken, as the water show dazzles the oblivious crowd. No words. No gestures. Just tension simmering in the air between them. Questions churn in her mind, each more frustrating than the last. *Why here? Why now?* But her gut tells her one thing-he isn't a threat. Not tonight.

Still, she keeps her defenses sharp, her posture steady, knowing better than to trust her instincts too deeply in a city where danger wears a thousand faces.

The show has ended; the sidewalk has become a flurry of tourists going in all different directions. The frenemy stranger makes his way towards her slowly. He stops a good twenty-five feet away. Smart man.

"My name is Lucas Williams. I am an Enforcer for the Humboldt Pack out of northern California."

Charlotte stays perfectly still, but her mind races. *What the fuck?* Why was he with those goons if he's not Cascade? Her wolf bristles inside, but Charlotte holds her tongue. Now's not the time for questions-just strategy. Of course, she has an exit plan. Always does.

With her back to the water, the fountains become her escape route. She could easily vault the wall and disappear into the spray, blending into the chaos. Sure, she'd end up in jail, but that's better than the alternative-killing a wolf in front of all these delicate humans. If she does that, her next stop won't be jail-it'll be a trial before the COPS.

Her eyes stay locked on him, her body ready for anything, but her mind is already running through every possible move.

"Hi, Lucas Williams," Charlotte says, her voice dripping with annoyance. "I'd introduce myself, but I'm guessing you already know my name-and everything else about me." Her eyes stay fixed on him, though her senses are on high alert, scanning for anything off. The Cascade Pack isn't exactly known for their creativity, so this could easily be another ambush. *Right here on the Strip?* It'd have a certain flair; she has to admit.

Lucas smirks, the kind that makes her want to punch him. "Not everything, She Alpha, but I know enough. Actually, it's what I know about our common enemy that brings us here. Miles Barlowe has a secret. One that would not only dethrone him, but that would be the lightest punishment he'd face."

Charlotte's eyebrow arches, curiosity creeping in despite herself. *This could be a trap,* she reminds herself, but her gut tells her Lucas might be telling the truth. "And why would you share this secret with me? How does it benefit my pack?"

Lucas' smirk doesn't waver. "No, Charlotte. I never said I was going to tell you the secret."

Her patience snaps, her fists clenching at her sides. "Then what the hell are we doing here? My time is valuable, and wasting it? That really pisses me off."

"Let's just say," Lucas pauses, his eyes narrowing as if calculating every word, "I have a newfound reason to keep your pack safe."

His expression shifts, something unreadable passing across his face. Charlotte studies him, trying to pin it down-empathy? Pity? No. It's something else, something she can't quite place.

"And I suppose that's a secret too?" Charlotte shoots back, her frustration barely contained.

"For now, yes," Lucas says evenly. "I'm not playing games, Charlotte. I hope for an alliance between our packs in the future, but for now, I have to keep these secrets close. I have a pack to think about, just like you do."

This whole exchange has Charlotte rattled, her mind spinning with questions. *What the hell is going on?* She suddenly realizes her guard has dropped. Her eyes flick around, taking in the scene-nothing's changed. The clueless humans keep shuffling along, arguing with their kids, couples holding hands as they move from one attraction to the next. Two bachelorette parties stagger by, laughing and shouting, completely oblivious.

"So," Charlotte begins, her voice sharp, "if you're part of-what did you call it? The Humboldt Pack? Why were you with those goons the other day?"

"The goons? That's fitting." Lucas chuckles, the sound grating on her nerves. "I've been with the Cascade Pack, gathering intel for a while now. That pack's been a pain in the ass for every other pack in Northern California. My pack and an ally decided we had to deal with them, without going to war. My loyalties are to my Alpha, Spencer Adler, and the Humboldt Pack. Trust me on that."

"A spy, then?" Charlotte's tone drips with suspicion.

Lucas pauses, his gaze calculating, weighing how much to tell her. "Yeah, you could call it that. But the spy game's about to end, and I'm hoping the Red Rock Pack will become an ally before it does."

And there it is—the deal. Charlotte feels the shift. The tension between them sharpens.

"So, if I agree to align the Red Rock Pack with the Humboldt's, you'll get shriveled-dick Miles off our backs?"

"Yes," Lucas replies, no hesitation.

"And how does this alignment benefit both our packs?" Charlotte's voice is tight, her skepticism rising. She won't be played.

Lucas meets her eyes, carefully choosing his next words. "I think you should meet my Alpha. Spencer wants to come here and talk to you himself. He'll need your permission to step into your territory."

Charlotte lets a slow smirk curl across her lips. "Yeah. My permission's a good idea if he wants to keep his skin."

She agrees to meet this Spencer, to have him come to Vegas for a face-to-face. Now that some of the mystery has peeled back, she wants more. She needs the details, the secret Lucas hinted at, and she's damn sure going to get it.

Lucas takes a step closer, his voice low and deliberate. "You'll want to hear what he has to say, Charlotte. It's bigger than just Miles... it's about the future of both our packs."

Charlotte's smirk fades. "You'd better hope it's worth my

time. If this is a waste, you and your Alpha will regret step-ping onto my territory."

Lucas's smirk returns, but his eyes flash with something unreadable. "Trust me, it'll be worth every second."

He gives a slight nod before disappearing into the crowd, leaving Charlotte standing by the fountains, the roar of water filling the silence that follows. Her mind churns with possibilities, but one thing's certain—this meeting is just the beginning.

JUST ONE BEER

After his conversation with Brian, Liam feels a little lighter. It's strange, realizing that even though he left his pack, they'd still welcome him back. There's a sense of relief, knowing that someone out there still cares, even if pack life no longer has a place in his future. It's not what he wants anymore, but the comfort lingers.

Standing at the "Do Not Walk" light with a mass of tourists, he catches the familiar spray of water misting through the air. The fountains are in full swing, dancing to *Viva Las Vegas*, lit up against the night sky. He takes in the scene, the chaos of Vegas swirling around him, when suddenly, it hits—hard. A familiar, intoxicating scent. One that's embedded itself in his thoughts and has no plans of leaving anytime soon.

No way.

Liam's eyes dart around, scanning the crowd like a predator stalking prey. But the source of his newfound fantasies is nowhere to be seen. The scent has his body reacting before his brain can catch up—his wolf stirred, his jeans tightening as the scent digs in.

"Well, well, if it isn't Liam Dunne, my knight in shining black fur."

Her voice—low, teasing—comes from behind him. Liam turns, and there she is. Charlotte, standing with her fists on her hips, a smirk playing on her lips, her perfectly trimmed brow lifting in challenge.

His knees almost buckle. His wolf perks up, pacing inside him. His body goes rigid, every nerve lit with awareness. *She's even more stunning than I remember.* His dick immediately takes notice, and for a second, he forgets how to breathe.

"Hey, Charlotte. I didn't think I'd ever see you again." *Except in my dreams*, he thinks but keeps that locked away.

Charlotte takes a slow step closer, the space between them humming with tension. "Well, I guess it's your lucky day. I never come to the Strip. You caught me on an off night." Her words are light, playful, but there's something deeper simmering under the surface.

Liam swallows hard, fighting the heat rising inside him. *Damn, this woman is beautiful.* His wolf is restless, but not in the usual growly, bitter way. No, this feels different—like a possessiveness he can't explain, shouldn't feel. But it's there, and it's dangerous.

"Well, Liam, I've got to get going. It was nice seeing you, and thanks again for saving my hide. Enjoy Vegas, but don't stay too long. The big bad she-wolf lives here," she says, her voice dipping into a playful growl.

She starts to turn, and it hits him that he's just standing there like an awkward troll, letting her walk away. *Fuck that.*

"Charlotte!" His voice comes out louder than he intended. She stops, turning slowly. "What would you say to having a beer with me? I mean, buying me a beer is the least you can do for saving your bacon." He throws on a smile, but inside, he's burning. What he *really* wants is to push her up against the nearest wall and make her scream his name right here on the Strip.

Charlotte pauses, her eyes flicking over him, a smirk still on her lips. "Sure. Why not?"

JUST ONE NIGHT

Holy balls. Charlotte can't believe it. The man who's consumed her thoughts for days is sitting across from her, perched on a barstool like it's the most natural thing in the world. This can't be good.

Her body reacts before her brain can catch up—little tingles racing across her skin just from the sight of his strong, work-worn hands resting on the counter. What the hell is up with these weird little giggles bubbling under the surface? She fights to keep them down, but it's a losing battle.

And now that she's not fighting for survival, she really sees him—the way his eyes sweep up and down her body, slow and deliberate, like he's undressing her in his mind. It's hot as hell, sending a rush straight to her core. Dammit, why didn't I just call Jason?

There's something about him, though. Playful, yes, but she senses the sadness underneath. She shouldn't care, shouldn't want to know more, but there's something about him that draws her in. No. This is a distraction. But... One night couldn't hurt, right?

Her gaze drifts to the small patches of grey at his temples, giving him that naughty professor vibe. She's already imagined him—four times now—with nothing but a tie and those round glasses, taking her from behind. His body, carved like a Greek god, is pure perfection. She vaguely hears him talking about his Bronco, but it's muffled. Her mind's busy with other things—like dragging her nails down those back muscles. Heat pools between her thighs. She shifts, but the friction of her leggings only makes it worse.

"So, Charlotte," Liam's voice snaps her out of her fantasy. "We've seen each other naked, but I don't even know your last name."

Her pre-orgasmic haze shatters. "Oh, it's Randolph. Charlotte Marie Randolph."

What the hell? Why did she give him her middle name, too?

She clears her throat, trying to recover. "I'm not great at small talk. My pack gives me shit about it all the time. Feels like a waste, and if I'm wasting time, I'm not making money."

"It's all business and no play for you, huh?" His words are more of a statement than a question. He takes a pull from his beer, then gestures toward the corner of the bar. "Check it out—there's a foosball table. Wanna kick my ass instead of sitting here awkwardly?"

Charlotte slides off her stool, grateful for the distraction. "Abso-fucking-lutely," she says, heading toward the table. Foosball isn't her game, but anything's better than thinking about how beautiful his dick probably is.

The first game is full of playful trash talk. Charlotte's not intimidated by his "I'm gonna kick your booty all the way to Timbuktu" shit-talk. But by the second and third games, something shifts. The small talk flows easier, more natural, and she finds herself having... *fun?*

"I really like your truck," Liam says, defending his goal with a focused grin.

"Thanks. The TRX is my dream truck. It's got all the power I need, and I can take it off-road whenever I want. I love hitting dirt roads, just to see what's on the other side of the hill."

"Same here. I've always loved exploring, even as a kid. I'd wander off, looking for bugs or shiny rocks, getting distracted by every new thing I found. I guess that's why becoming a lone wolf wasn't as hard for me as I thought it would be."

Charlotte pauses mid-shot, her curiosity piqued. "Why are you a lone wolf?" The question slips out before she can stop it. "Sorry, I didn't mean to—"

"No, it's okay." Liam takes a deep breath, his expression shifting. "I had a good pack. I loved them and they loved me but there was an accident that changed me forever."

The words hang heavy in the air, charged with a power that makes Charlotte's wolf stir.

"I tried to adjust to pack life after that, but it didn't work. I left, planning to be gone for a month or two... that turned into seven. Turns out being alone wasn't as hard as I expected."

There's a weight in his voice; a quiet strength Charlotte recognizes—the same power she felt during the battle. It's Alpha power, but controlled, tempered in a way she's never experienced before. As his words sink in, everything around them fades—the loud chatter, the clinking of glasses, even the music pumping through the bar. It all dissolves into the background, leaving just the two of them. The moment stretches, thick with truth and unspoken pain.

For once, her wolf isn't pacing or snarling. She's still, almost... content. It's a strange but welcome calm, one that settles into Charlotte's bones, warming her from the inside out. Her wolf, normally on edge around any male, feels something different—something she hasn't felt in years or maybe ever. Peace. The steady hum of a connection between them quiets the usual chaos, and for a split second, it's like the world outside doesn't exist.

It's just Liam, his power rolling off him like a wave, and Charlotte, grounded in a way she never expected. She feels-safe.

As the calm settles in, Charlotte feels something unsettling tug at her. Vulnerability. It's not something she's allowed herself to feel, especially not with a male. She's the Alpha Female, the one in control, the one making decisions. Yet here she is, letting her guard slip, and her wolf—normally bristling at the proximity of a male—is at ease. It feels too easy, and that scares her.

What is this? she wonders, torn between letting the moment last and pulling herself out of it. The air between them thickens, but her thoughts are already spinning out, looking for the exit. She knows better than to trust this calm—knows better than to let someone in, especially someone who could be more than a distraction. But right now, she doesn't want to move.

Mate, her wolf whispers, the word sending a ripple of calm through her, a stark contrast to the constant tension that's always been her companion.

No. We don't get one of those, Charlotte snaps back, trying to smother the spark before it ignites. *Fuck you, wolf. We've got more important things to focus on.* Her wolf only hums in response, content, completely ignoring the chaos swirling in Charlotte's mind. With a battle looming. A pack to protect.

She can't afford this kind of distraction. Her wolf should be pacing, growling, resisting. But instead, her wolf settles.

Him. The word echoes calmly, sinking through her mind, so at odds with the tension knotting her every thought. Charlotte isn't used to this peace—especially not now.

And damn it, Liam's presence pulls at her in a way she can't quite shake.

Suddenly, the world rushes back in—loud voices, the clatter of pint glasses, the slam of liquor bottles being dropped into wells. It rattles her, her guard shooting back up. She glances over her shoulder, suddenly hyperaware of her surroundings.

Liam exhales, as if a weight has been lifted. "Wow, I've never said that out loud before. Feels... good."

"Thanks for telling me." The words come out harsher than she intended, and it grates on her. Something inside twists, an unfamiliar urge to shield him from any more hurt, which makes no sense. She doesn't do this—doesn't get involved in other people's pain. Unless they are pack. But now, knowing the sadness that clings to him, something in her stirs. The power she felt radiating from him fades, but the weight of his truth hangs heavy, making her feel exposed. And she hates that more than anything.

Liam's smile returns, softer this time. "For someone who drives a badass truck and owns a gym, you're terrible at foosball. Gotta admit, I had higher expectations, Charlotte Marie Randolph."

She laughs despite herself. "That's it, no more holding back." She slides the ball through the serving hole, determination lighting up her face.

After a few more rounds—none of which Charlotte wins—they settle back at the high-top table. The night flows easily, full of laughter about stupid tourists, the annoyance of coyote shifters, and why the color red is just plain irritating.

Their beers are almost empty, but Charlotte doesn't want the night to end. Without thinking, she blurts out, "What hotel are you staying at?"

Liam's eyebrows shoot up, a playful grin spreading across his face. "Why? You wanna see my bed, Charlotte?" He wiggles his eyebrows, his nerdy awkwardness shining through. "It's off the Strip, just a few blocks. I walked over. Mind giving me a ride back?"

Charlotte swallows the last of her beer, her heart racing. "Absolutely." She tells herself she'll just drop him off and leave.

Yup. Just giving him a ride back.

FUCK

Liam can't help himself. Sure, he could've walked back to the hotel, but being around Charlotte was too much fun—too easy. He can't remember the last time he laughed like that, the kind of deep, belly laugh that comes from actually feeling comfortable. She's has this sarcastic, dry sense of humor that matches his nerdy quirks perfectly, and for the first time in a long time, it feels... natural.

Even his wolf had been calm at the bar, something that rarely happens. The wolf had hung on every word Charlotte said, quietly absorbing her energy. But now, in the confines of her truck, both the man and the wolf are wide awake. He's hyper-aware of the heat radiating from her body, of how close they are, and it's taking every ounce of restraint not to slide his hand onto her thigh.

"I think you turn here," he says, pointing to a familiar street. She flicks on the blinker and pulls into the old motel lot. It's one of those Vegas places that tries to look glamorous, with its mirrored canopy and oversized bulbs casting a golden glow over everything. It's tacky, but it works.

"This is it. My room's just past the lobby." His heart is pounding. The moment feels heavy, like something's about to shift.

She parks the truck in front of the hotel, the engine's growl fading as if the moment itself is holding its breath. The tires crunch against the loose-gravel, and the soft glow from the headlights spills out over the pavement, highlighting the hotel's entrance like a spotlight. His pulse quickens, matching the fading vibration of the truck. He notices her fingers grip the steering wheel, holding on a little longer than necessary, like she's holding on to something more.

This is it. Now or never. His nerves are electric, buzzing beneath his skin. With a breath that feels too shallow, he turns in his seat to face her. His voice barely steady, he meets her gaze. "I'm going to be completely honest. I want you to stay. I want you."

It's like a dam breaking. Before he can second-guess himself, he leans in and presses his lips to hers, soft at first—testing. *Oh fuck,* her lips are even softer than he imagined. He pulls back just a fraction, wanting to see her reaction, but she's already on him, grabbing the back of his neck and pulling him into a kiss that's harder, needier.

Liam's pulse kicks up as her lips part, letting him explore her mouth, and for a second, it feels like every fantasy he's had about her just collided with reality. Her skin is warm under his hands, softer than he could've dreamed, and he can't help but wrap his hand around the back of her neck, pulling her closer.

Her scent—God, her scent—is driving him insane, erasing every bit of control he thought he had. She deepens the kiss, a clear signal that she's giving him what he's been craving. He takes his chance, slipping his hand under her purple tank top. Her bra is smooth and silky beneath his palm. The soft moan she lets out when his thumb grazes her nipple sends a jolt of pleasure straight through him, making his dick ache with need.

Charlotte leans into him, pressing against his hand, and he gives her a gentle squeeze, rewarded by another moan— a sound that is now his new favorite thing. It's like they've been at it for hours, making out in her truck like a couple of teenagers. He's lost track of time.

It doesn't matter. Nothing does, except the way she responds to his touch, the way her pleasure feels like his only purpose in this moment.

He's about to suggest taking this to his room, when the shrill ring of her phone cuts through the haze.

Charlotte drops her head against his shoulder with a frustrated groan. "Fuck."

Liam can't agree more. *Fuck.*

HAPPY TIME

Charlotte can't believe the timing of this phone call. Seriously, someone better have lost an arm, because right now, she needs this man. *No.* She clenches her teeth. *No, that can't be right.* She needs her pack. She needs her truck. She needs her gym. This man? He's a release. Nothing more. Nothing less. But even as she tries to convince herself of that, her wolf snarls low in her chest, a warning that sends a shiver up her spine.

Her fingers fumble behind her neck, fighting with the pocket between her shoulder blades to yank out her phone. It rings again. Twice now, and her irritation spikes with each shrill tone. She doesn't even glance at the screen before jabbing the answer button. "One of you better be dead, because you just interrupted happy time," she snaps.

Out of the corner of her eye, she catches Liam shifting in his seat, straightening like he's bracing for something. She threw too much power behind that, and even though it wasn't meant for him, she regrets it.

"I don't want to know about your happy time, Charlotte," Lucas's voice crackles through the line, his chuckle grating against her nerves. "Spencer's heading to Vegas on Friday. Where do you want to meet She-Alpha?"

Charlotte's gaze flicks to Liam, knowing full well he can hear every word. Her stomach tightens. She doesn't need him more entangled in her pack's mess than he already is. "Let me talk to the pack and I'll call you back," she mutters, cutting the call short.

Shifting in the seat, thoughts wrestle for control. *Get it together.* "Liam, this has been fun, but it's probably best to stop things now. You're cute, but there's a lot going on right now."

A quick glance toward him, searching for any sign of reaction. The rapid thudding in her chest betrays the calm tone. *Does he care? Why do I care if he cares? What the fuck Charlotte?*

Liam's face remains calm, thoughtful, no sign of being rattled. "I didn't realize you were the Alpha. You're quite the enigma, Charlotte Randolph."

Her breath catches, not at the words but the way he says them—like he sees her, really sees her. "Yeah?" She swallows down the frustration rising in her chest. "Liam Dunne, you hide your alpha animal well, but I feel him. There's more to your story too, isn't there?" The question falls out sharper than she intends, and for a moment, she wonders why she's mad.

He just smiles, disarming and boyish, that stupid smile that makes her stomach twist. "Thanks for the beers. I had a great time in Vegas, but I'll be out of your territory soon."

Liam picks up his phone, fingers tapping rapidly across the screen. A soft chime sounds between them, followed by a gentle buzz in her lap. Glancing down, the screen lights up with his contact card.

"Just in case you need me." His voice is light, teasing.

"You never know when you'll need someone to kick your ass at foosball, you know, to keep you humbled." The shy smile that follows makes something flutter inside her.

Stop that.

He reaches out, his hand wrapping around hers, warm and solid. "Stay safe, Charlotte."

Before she can think of a response, he slides out of the truck, giving her a casual two-finger wave over his shoulder as he disappears behind the sliding doors of his hotel.

The second he's gone, a hollow feeling creeps in, leaving her empty. *This shouldn't be happening. He's just a nerd. A very sexy, super-smart nerd that can kisses like he invented the damn concept and forgot to tell the rest of the world.* Her chest tightens, and she swallows the unfamiliar ache. She misses him.

YUP. THE ENEMY OF MY ENEMY
IS DEFINITELY AN ASSHOLE

F riday arrives too fast, a day looming like a dark
cloud Charlotte isn't ready for. Sitting on the hot-
pink leather of the L-shaped couch, she leans over
the glass-top table, narrowing her eyes at the ice buckets.
Glass tables? Again? Irritation simmers beneath the surface,
but a quick nod to the cocktail server confirms the setup is
correct, even if everything else feels wrong.

"I'll return when your guests arrive, Charlotte." The
brunette server spins on her heel and disappears through
the elevator doors, leaving Charlotte alone with her
thoughts, the rising tension clinging to the air like static.

The zebra-print lamp throws a soft white glow that
clashes with the deep purples radiating from the ceiling.
Crimson Moon—the hottest and most exclusive nightclub
in Las Vegas—was chosen for a reason. This isn't just any
club; it's Willamena's domain, owned and protected by the
Nightshade Coven. The burlesque-themed fortress draped
in velvet and neon is not only the center of Vegas nightlife,
but a stronghold for vampires who rule these dark corners.

Below, dancers glide across the stage, draped in lace,

while the crowd thrashes under the pulsing rhythm of the music. But Charlotte's mind isn't on the show. It's on the meeting. It's on the threat.

The vampires have always been elusive, operating on the fringes of the shifters' world. Willamena and her coven know nearly everything about the shifters, yet Charlotte's pack knows precious little about them—an advantage Willamena holds with deadly precision. If things with Spencer go sideways tonight, Charlotte has no choice but to trust that Willamena and her vamps will back them up. At least, that's the hope.

Lifting the martini to her lips, she savors the slow burn as it rolls down her throat, a sharp reminder that she's still alive, still in control. The glass swirled with red, mimicking blood, is a signature touch. *Of course they'd do this,* she smirks. *Always the dramatics with vampires.* The humor is brief, quickly replaced by the weight of what's coming.

Across from her, Jade fidgets, tension rolling off her in waves. "So, again, this Lucas guy didn't attack you? At all?" Her voice is sharp, fingers absentmindedly spinning a small curved blade, the weapon practically an extension of her hand. "Just tossed you around like a rag doll, made it look like he was with the Cascades? Then somehow got your number and set up this meeting with his Alpha? And now we're just sitting here—in a vampire den—waiting for him to show?"

Jade's eyes flick toward the elevator, her grip tightening around the polished wood handle of her knife. "I don't like it. None of it."

"Jade, you don't like *anything*," Charlotte replies, though her own unease mirrors Jade's. The stem of her glass presses into her palm. "But I get it. I don't know what this is really about either. Lucas didn't seem hostile, but who knows what their angle is." Another sip of the martini barely calms her racing thoughts. "Our numbers are low. Recruitment isn't happening fast enough. If this is about allyship, maybe it'll buy us temporary protection."

Her gaze shifts to the dancefloor below, where lights flash in time with the deep thrum of the bass. "And we're here because Willamena won't let anything go down in her club. She's the wild card we need."

Before Jade can respond, the elevator pings softly, doors sliding open to reveal Harper and Luna. Their infectious energy spills into the VIP area as they step out, practically vibrating with excitement. Luna's still bopping her head to the music, moving as though the club's pulse courses through her veins.

"Hot damn!" Luna grins, taking in the space. "Why don't we come here more often? This place is hotter than a MILF on divorce day."

Charlotte releases a breath she hadn't realized she'd been holding. Their arrival grounds her, but the protectiveness still coils inside, sharp and on edge. *This isn't just a night out. This is a chess game, and every piece has to be in place.* If Spencer turns out to be more threat than ally, she'll need to act fast—faster than anyone sees coming.

Harper grabs a gothic-inspired rocks glass, downing the fruity red contents in one swift motion. "Hey, Char, there's a guy on the dance floor you might want to check out. Definitely your type. Looks like that wrestler you always get googly-eyed over. What's his name again? Starts with an R... Ray? Ralph? Radrick?"

"*Roman*," Charlotte corrects, huffing. "And I do *not* get googly." A few weeks ago, the mention of a Roman look-alike would've had her prowling the dance floor, ready to pounce. Tonight, though? It turns her stomach.

The anxiety bubbling beneath the surface spikes higher. *It's the meeting,* she tells herself, *that's what's off.* It's definitely *not* the fact that a certain six-foot-five nerd has been taking up far too much space in her mind lately. Definitely not that.

"Let's just get through this damn meeting," she mutters, though the words ring hollow even to her own ears. That kiss was enough—a dangerous glimpse of what letting Liam in might mean. The thought of never wanting him to leave gnaws at her edges, threatening her focus. But tonight, there's no room for those feelings, no space for distractions.

Movement on the dance floor below draws her attention. Silas, leading four large men toward the mirrored elevator. A quick scan left and right confirms her suspicions —Silas would never expose his back to wolves without proper security. Elena, blending in effortlessly with the crowd, holds position on his right, while Lazarus mirrors her on the left. From a distance, they look like any other humans out for a good time, but their presence speaks volumes.

As the elevator doors slide open again, Silas and his entourage step into the VIP area, approaching the most coveted table in all of Las Vegas. The four men behind him radiate strength, but it's the cold, calculated way they move that sends a ripple of unease through her. Every movement is deliberate, as if they've already sized up every exit, every threat.

"Charlotte," Silas greets, his voice smooth but edged with a warning. "Your VIP guests have arrived. I don't need to remind you that the happiness of our... patrons is of utmost importance to Willamena. So, please refrain from disrupting the ecstasy coursing through every human vein. I trust you'll explain the rules to your new friends?"

His eyes lock onto hers for a brief moment before he

steps back toward the elevator. The weight of the unspoken rules presses heavy on her chest.

Lucas, along with three very large men—two of whom look like brothers—stands at the table. "Let's make this easy, Charlotte. This is Spencer, my Alpha, and these are Kai and Jaxson, both Humboldt Enforcers."

The men nod toward the women, and Spencer extends his hand.

Standing, Charlotte shakes his hand, her eyes never leaving his. "I'm not sure yet if it's nice to meet you. The one and only rule is, no violence in the club. If even one drop of blood hits the floor, that human or shifter will die. Vamps have a lot of control, but when they're packed into a club with this much adrenaline, hormones, and pheromones, they tend to get... amped. So do not cause any deaths. Questions?"

Four heads shake in unison.

"Perfect," Charlotte begins, gesturing to the women beside her. "This is Jade and Harper, both Enforcers of the Red Rock Pack. And Luna—let's just say she's the baddest of the badasses."

A proud smirk tugs at her lips. She can feel the subtle shift in the air as all three women lift their chins just slightly, confidence rolling off them in waves. "And I am the Alpha of this all-female pack."

She motions to the table, the tension crackling between them like static. "I took the liberty of ordering several bottles. I didn't know what everyone drinks."

Spencer's voice booms across the table, though his tone stays civil. "Thank you. That's very generous."

Lucas rises, his movements deliberate as he hands beer bottles to the other men, but Charlotte catches the flicker of something in his expression—like he's scanning the room for threats, or maybe weaknesses. A predator assessing prey.

The brunette server rushes back in, breathless. "I'm sorry, I got tied up next door." She quickly refills the ladies' glasses, but Charlotte can't afford any distractions right now.

Taking the glass from her, Charlotte's voice is firm but polite. "It's fine. We'll take care of ourselves for the rest of the evening. We need complete privacy." The young girl nods, bowing her head slightly before retreating.

Eyes narrowing, Charlotte's attention returns to the table. Something feels off. Harper and Lucas exchange a fleeting glance, too quick to catch the details, but it sends a ripple of suspicion through her. *Did that just happen?*

Before she can dwell on it, Spencer speaks, cutting through the mounting tension.

"Charlotte, we share a mutual enemy. Miles Barlowe has been a stain on our kind for years. He's terrorized the Pacific Northwest packs, and we've tried to get the COPS involved. But you know they don't care unless humans are affected, and Miles is careful—too careful. Now that he's moved to a new territory, we can't sit by any longer. We need to stop him. Several bear clans are already viewing us as weak. And while I'm not afraid to fight them, war is last resort."

Jade's scoff cuts through the air like a blade. "If he's been such a problem, why didn't you take care of him before?" Her tone is sharp, biting, laced with challenge.

Charlotte shoots her a warning look. It's a legitimate question, but this isn't the time for Jade's usual bite. Control needs to stay in her hands. "Jade," Charlotte's voice is low, dripping with cold authority. "We're going to listen for now. Let's give our *new frenemies* a chance to explain why these assholes have gone unchecked while our pack suffered losses, all while they worked to gather their precious intel."

The disdain in her voice is unmistakable, and Spencer's gaze drops slightly, the weight of guilt softening his features. "We are truly sorry for your losses," he murmurs, sincerity heavy in his tone. "We knew the Cascades had gone quiet, but until we heard whispers of an all-female pack defending Las Vegas, we had no idea where Miles had moved his focus. You have our utmost respect and condolences."

Charlotte's eyes harden, though she gives a curt nod. "Thank you. But let's get to it. Why would you reveal your secret to help us? And what's so powerful about this secret that it would force Miles to abandon his pursuit of revenge?"

Spencer shifts in his seat, his focus now on all four women. "Are you aware of how Miles came to be the Alpha of the Cascade Pack?"

The silence thickens as the women exchange glances. Charlotte breaks it. "No. We just know he's a relentless pig, willing to sacrifice anyone and anything when his fragile ego gets bruised."

Spencer's expression darkens as he leans forward. "Miles was the runt of the pack growing up."

Luna cuts in, rolling her eyes. "Well, that explains a lot."

Spencer pauses to take a drink of his beer, seemingly unfazed by Luna's interruption. When it's clear she won't add more, he continues. "But it's not what you think. He wasn't the typical bullied runt. In fact, it was the opposite. His parents treated him like he was untouchable, and the pack rallied around him, making sure he always felt big, strong—invincible. As we all got older—"

"Wait. What?" Charlotte and Jade speak in unison, cutting him off, suspicion thick in the air.

"Yes," Spencer begins, his voice low and measured. "Miles was a Redwood. We all grew up together. He's three years younger than us," he gestures toward Kai and Jaxson before shifting his gaze to Lucas, "but he and Lucas were best friends growing up. That connection made it easy for Lucas to integrate into the Cascade Pack."

Charlotte's eyes flick to Lucas. He drops his gaze to the floor, as if carrying the weight of Miles's wrongdoings. Guilt hangs in the air like a thick fog, pressing down on him.

Jade, leaning back in her chair, lets out a sigh, her expression bored. "I sure hope this story time is leading to the secret that'll keep me from killing more Cascades. My wolf's developed quite the taste for it." She gives her signature "meh" face, entirely unimpressed by the Miles biography unfolding before them.

Despite the shock that Miles was once a Redwood, Charlotte struggles to care. This backstory feels too distant from the present threat looming over her pack.

"I'll get to it," Spencer replies, unshaken by Jade's impatience. "If I don't give you the context, you'd just ask all these questions anyway."

Lucas seizes the pause, rising from his seat. "Does anyone need a refill?" His attempt to break the tension is met with a few head shakes before all eyes return to Spencer.

Spencer continues, his voice steady but laced with something darker.

"As we grew up, Miles became more arrogant. He'd challenge me constantly, always trying to prove something." Lucas leans back slightly, jaw tightening like he's watching the memories play out in front of him. "I didn't want to hurt him. He was like a brother, so I'd go easy on him. And he knew it."

A humorless huff slips out of him.

"That only fueled his anger. Part of him knew he'd never win if I truly fought back. By the time we hit our twenties, it was clear he was growing bitter. Hostile." His fingers drum once against the arm of the chair before going still. "He'd make snide remarks about how he should be Alpha, how the Adler family had cheated in the past to win the throne. His great-grandfather lost in a challenge, or so the story went."

Spencer's jaw tightens as he speaks, and Charlotte catches the briefest flicker of pain in his eyes.

"I loved Miles. So, when my father handed down the Alpha role to me, I went to Miles and asked him to prove the deception he claimed."

His hand tightens once against his knee before releasing.

"It would have been the hardest thing I'd ever done, but if my family had cheated, I would've stepped down."

He pauses, his voice growing quieter. "But he couldn't. No proof. Nothing solid. Just his father's word, and every time I pressed for details, he'd deflect. No straight answers. Just anger."

Charlotte studies Spencer's face, noticing the lines of tension, the weight of the past that still clings to him. He's trying to be stoic, but the pain bleeds through. His words are heavy, burdened with memories he can't shake. He takes a drink, the pause lingering in the air.

"So how did Miles become Alpha of the Cascade Pack?" Charlotte leans in, her tone sharp. "We heard that before him, the Cascades were fair, friendly. They were even starting to treat women better."

Spencer's gaze drops—a subtle, almost imperceptible shift, but enough to jolt Charlotte. *Alphas don't lower their eyes.* Whatever this question touched, it's deep. Painful.

Slowly, he raises his head, but the weight of the emotion still lingers.

"Miles issued an official challenge," Spencer says, the words dragging out of him. "I had no choice but to accept. Everyone knew it wasn't going to be a fair fight. Even Miles knew it. But what we didn't know at the time was that he had a plan to tip the scales in his favor."

The story, as much as it irritates Charlotte, is becoming more intriguing. The pieces are falling into place, but her patience is wearing thin. *There had better be a secret,* she thinks, suppressing the urge to interrupt. She's always been more of a *read-the-last-page-first* kind of girl, and this slow burn is grating on her nerves.

"Kai and Jaxson were doing security checks the night before the challenge. They came across Miles and another member of our pack that is no longer breathing." Spencer stopped there and looked over at the two brothers.

Jaxson speaks calmly, his tone steady, almost detached, as if nothing can shake him. "We asked him why he was in the kitchen that late and what the hell was that powder? Then everything went to hell."

"Before we knew it, the kitchen was destroyed, Kyle was dead, and I had Miles in custody," Kai says with innocence. He is by far the largest of the large men, so the tenderness when he spoke was unexpected.

Spencer's voice is steady, but there's a heaviness in it, the weight of someone who's seen too much. "We called in some friends to test the powder that night. Turns out, it was a chemical designed to weaken a shifter, nearly shutting down the healing process. The council uses it on out-of-control shifters, but it's illegal for anyone else to have." He pauses, taking a slow drink from his beer, as if bracing himself before continuing. "We contacted the council right away. They came, confirmed it was their powder, and launched an investigation. But it didn't go far. Miles... he lied his way out of it."

The frustration in his voice is subtle, buried beneath the surface, but the disappointment lingers, a reminder of the burden he carries for his pack.

"Once again," Charlotte begins, the exasperation clear in her voice, "this is all very interesting, and it proves beyond a shadow of a doubt that Miles is an asshat. But that secret? It won't protect us."

"No," Lucas interjects, his tone calm but carrying weight. "But the fact that he used the same poison to win the Cascade throne will."

The room seems to still. *Now that is something.*

"If the rest of the Cascades found out their Alpha is nothing but a spoiled-brat who cheated his way into power?" Spencer's eyes bore into Charlotte's, the intensity in his gaze unwavering. "It would set everything on fire."

Charlotte holds his stare, her mind racing. A slow smile tugs at the corner of her mouth, edged with sarcasm. "Well, shit. That's a nice secret to have, isn't it? Now, what's the catch? I doubt you're handing over this little nugget with zero expectations."

Spencer pauses, taking a slow drink from his beer. Charlotte can see the wheels turning behind those calm eyes, his careful consideration of every word before it's spoken.

"Ah, so there *is* a catch."

"I know Lucas already mentioned the idea of aligning our packs," Spencer begins, his voice measured, deliberate. "I told you the whole story hoping you'd at least consider my proposal."

With that, Spencer sets down a glass jar filled with dark

soil. It takes Charlotte a second to realize what it is. *Dirt from his den.* The meaning is unmistakable, a tradition that stretches back through centuries. When a male chooses a female, he offers earth from his den as a symbol of his commitment. Shock roots her in place.

"Proposal?" Jade's voice breaks through the air just as the music cuts off. "As in *mating*?" Her exclamation reverberates through the sudden silence, snapping Charlotte out of her daze.

What the hell? Charlotte's glare sharpens. "What, did all your other allies turn down your marriage proposals? It doesn't take mating to form an alliance."

Spencer doesn't flinch, his gaze steady and unyielding. "You're right. You don't need a husband to keep your pack safe. But strength alone won't save you, Charlotte. Your pack is small—vulnerable. I'm offering you a way out of that vulnerability."

Charlotte's wolf bristles, but she keeps her voice measured. "And I suppose you think I should just accept your terms without question? Trust you implicitly?"

He leans back in his chair, his lips curling into a faint smirk. "I think you'd be smart to. You've already lost wolves. How many more are you willing to lose before you admit you need help?"

Her grip on the glass tightens, the stem digging into her palm. "Watch your words, Spencer. Carefully."

He shrugs, unfazed. "I'm not here to make friends or coddle egos. I'm here because we share an enemy who's gaining strength while your pack dwindles. I've already done the math, Charlotte. You're running out of time."

Charlotte's jaw tightens, but before she can fire back, Spencer presses on. "And then there's the powder."

The words land with a chilling weight, silencing the

room. Her wolf's ears metaphorically perk, alert and poised for a fight. Charlotte narrows her eyes, keeping her voice calm. "What about it?"

Spencer leans forward, his smirk replaced by something... else."You think Miles stopped using it after he took the Cascade Pack? You think your losses are just from bad luck and stronger wolves? You've seen how he fights—dirty, ruthless, always with an edge no one else seems to have."

The words hit like a blade to the chest, and Charlotte struggles to keep her reaction in check. Her mind races through every recent loss, every injury that lingered longer than it should have. Could it be true?

"I'll show you the proof," Spencer continues, his voice low. "But only if you're ready to do what's necessary. This isn't just about alliances, Charlotte. It's about survival."

The tension in the room is suffocating, the air crackling with unspoken threats. Jade shifts in her seat, her knife spinning idly between her fingers. Luna leans back, her grin sharp and amused, while Harper's eyes narrow, watching Spencer like a hawk.

Charlotte straightens, her voice cold. "We don't mate for politics. My pack doesn't need your charity or your alliances. If you think you're calling the shots here, let me remind you whose territory you're standing in."

Spencer leans forward again, his tone soft but laced with steel. "Then prove it. Show me that you're more than a desperate Alpha clinging to a losing hand. Because right now, I see someone who's strong—but not strong enough."

The words hit like a blow, but Charlotte refuses to flinch. She doesn't break eye contact, the challenge in his gaze met with equal force.

Luna's voice breaks the tension like a needle to a balloon. "You know, for someone who wants an alliance, you've got a really shitty way of asking for it. Maybe a fruit basket next time?"

Charlotte doesn't laugh. She doesn't take her eyes off Spencer. "We'll see how strong you think I am by the end of this conversation."

ARE YOU OUT OF MY TERRITORY

"Well, isn't this some bullshit?" Charlotte mutters, standing in the middle of her black metallic-tiled shower. This room was picked for a reason—the overindulgent bathroom. The wall behind, covered in oversized earthy tiles of browns and greens, makes the space feel grounded, but it's the rainfall showerhead above that offers the real escape. Hot water pours down, but no matter how scalding it is, it doesn't burn off the mess from the Crimson Moon. It keeps playing on a loop in her head—the secret, the proposal, the pressure.

A mating would strengthen the packs, sure, but is it necessary? Other packs manage fine with simple fealty. There's no need for all this... complication.

The Red Rocks left with only a vague *we'll get back to you,* and Charlotte knows it's her decision in the end. But it affects everyone. So, the pack will have to work this out. There's no way around that.

Her wolf stirs beneath the surface, restless, irritated. That damn proposal shook them all. It's clear now that a pack run is overdue—for her and the others. The bond between them has to stay strong, and nothing reinforces it like shifting. Their wolves need to feel each other, run together, move as one. It's the only way to keep the connection, to ensure their strength remains unbreakable.

But no matter how much the pack needs her focus, something else keeps slipping through the cracks. Spencer's proposal, the jar on the table—it was meant to strengthen the pack, but it brought something else to the surface, something Charlotte didn't expect. Liam. His presence edges into her thoughts, uninvited. *Why is the first instinct to call him?* The question gnaws at her, tugging at the fragile balance between pack responsibilities and something far more personal. The news she received could keep the pack safe, but the cost? It's one that money can't touch.

Stepping out of the shower, Charlotte reaches for the fluffy purple towel—a recent addition that screamed "Isabell." Luna had brought Isabell in just a few days ago to help with the house, and already her presence was making ripples. It wasn't just that she was friendly to the non-human world; it was the way she moved through it like she belonged. Like she understood.

The royal purple towels were one example, a small luxury Charlotte hadn't known she needed until it was there. And then there were the details—like the stash of Flavorblasted Goldfish that mysteriously appeared in the pantry. Isabell seemed to have a knack for anticipating needs, even in a house she barely knew.

She hadn't been with them long enough to earn trust outright, but there was something about her quiet confidence, the way she instinctively knew when to step in or give space, that hinted at a deeper understanding. Charlotte couldn't quite place it yet, but she had the feeling Isabell wasn't just a housekeeper—she was something more.

Still, no amount of fluff or goldfish could distract from the thoughts swirling in Charlotte's mind. Reaching for the phone on the countertop, she hovers a finger above Liam's contact, indecision churning. A deep breath steadies her, and before another thought can stop her, the message icon is tapped.

> Are you out of my territory?

The text sends before regret can settle in fully. Setting the phone down, there's no time to dwell before three little dots appear. Charlotte had no idea three dots could spark such relief.

> Hey, beautiful! I was just thinking about you.

Scooping the phone back up, the flood of warmth is instant. Those eight little words are enough to smooth the rough edges of the day. *Beautiful.* Maybe it's okay to need to feel that—just for a minute. And he's long gone, no longer an addictive temptation waiting just down the road.

> Yeah? I saw a nerd walking down the street,
> so I thought about you too.

A moment passes before his reply comes through, quick and teasing.

> A nerd made you think of me? He must've been a damn sexy nerd then. A grinning emoji with nerd glasses finishes the text.

Couldn't be sexier than you, she thinks but leaves unsaid. Instead, fingers type something safer.

How far did you make it?

> Not far. I thought I'd see the Grand Canyon
> while I was in the area. This thing is
> incredible!

Attached is a selfie with the canyon in the background. Instead of the little shy smile Charlotte has seen a few times now, he has the biggest cheesy smile she has ever seen on anyone. It's like the nerd found nerd heaven and is doing nerd-heavenly things. She will never forget the shirt he had on the day they met. She will think about that smile as she does naughty things to herself later.

Yeah, it's pretty damn impressive. I've been
there a few times. What lookout is that?

It takes Liam a second to respond.

> I took so many I don't even remember which
> one that was at. You should come down
> here and we'll figure it out together.

Charlotte skirts that one and types,

You know that attack that happened in the
gym parking lot?

> You mean the one where I killed a guy? I
> vaguely remember that, yeah.

Those guys are from the Cascade Pack.
They came to claim Vegas for the first time
about three years ago. Since then, we have
fought four battles, where we have lost
eleven pack members.

Charlotte lowers the phone for a second, drawing in a

slow breath that burns all the way down like grief still remembers where to live.

> Today, I received an offer that could ensure the safety of what we have left and secure our territory, but it will cost me my freedom.

Charlotte hesitates, but hits send. She is unsure if unloading on an almost stranger is wise, but she can't seem to help herself.

> What was the offer, and why you?

Charlotte just sits for a minute to think about the answer. What did she think would happen? He wouldn't ask questions?

"Fucking brilliant Charlotte. What now?" She asks herself.

> It's a long story. Too long for texting.

She hits send and hopes that he'll leave it at that. She hears "IDGAF" play on her phone. It's her ringtone for anyone that isn't programmed. She knows she won't get away with *Oops. Sorry I didn't hear it,* trick. "Fuck!" She hits the little green phone. "Hey."

"Hear me out. From my point of view, I have all night and all day. I can even go into the next day. I am *that* available to you. After that, we'll have to negotiate compensation for my time." There's a teasing lilt in Liam's voice that sends a ripple through her, pulling her in further. "But right now, I'm all yours. Since we've already seen each other naked and you ravished my mouth, I think talking is the next step in this relationship."

That voice. It wraps around her, warm and electric, doing dangerous things to her mind. The calm should unnerve her, but it doesn't. Instead, it amplifies everything, like she's teetering on a precipice. *Why is this different?* It's the trust. That's what scares her most. She's never trusted men easily, and yet... with him? It feels natural.

"All night and all day? That's some stamina, Liam Dunne." Flirting feels safer, an easy escape from the harder things, the heavy things. The things that make her want to run. But right now, she doesn't want the call to end.

"Oh, Charlotte, let me tell you, the things I've thought about doing to you would make a *great* screenplay for a blue movie," his voice drops, smoky and low.

Heat rushes through her so fast it almost stings. *Well, that escalated quickly.* She rarely blushes, but right now, it feels like the air itself is on fire. That one sentence sends a pulse straight to her core. Her clit throbs, nipples pebbling under the soft towel she's barely aware of anymore. At some point, she ended up sitting at the edge of her bed, knees weak with need.

Play, her mind whispers. *What's the harm?*

"Really?" Her voice comes out sultry, teasing. "And what sort of things have you done to me, Liam?"

That voice again, low and confident, washes over her. "It started at dinner."

Charlotte cuts him off, playing with him. "Boring."

"I am not even close to done with you, Charlotte," Liam's voice hardens, and her entire body reacts. A shudder runs through her as her pussy clenches tight at the sound. There's a dominance in his tone she wasn't expecting, and her wolf—usually quick to challenge—is unnervingly quiet. It's as if even her animal instincts are submitting to him, allowing him this power. *Why him?*

Why does he get to speak to her this way and not provoke her usual fire?

Liam clears his throat, and the sensual control in his voice returns. "Like I was saying, we started dinner at Consciousness."

Her brows rise. *Consciousness.* The restaurant where senses are stripped away, one by one. Blindfolds, noise-canceling headphones, touch heightened by the absence of sight and sound. The most sensual dining experience in the world, designed to overwhelm the body.

"How the fuck do you know about Consciousness? That place isn't exactly on the Vegas tourist map." Charlotte's surprise slips out before she can stop it.

Liam chuckles, back to his usual voice. "I'm a nerd, remember? I know how to do my research."

Damn, that smile. She can feel it, even over the phone. He's unlike anyone she's ever been drawn to, and she's still figuring out what to do with that.

"Now stop interrupting my story," Liam says, his teasing tone back in place. "You asked about my fantasy, and I'm trying to share." Then his voice drops again, seductive and intimate, pulling her deeper. "Storytime, Charlotte. Just sit back and relax. We finish dinner, and I've got a surprise for you. You hate surprises, so this is driving you crazy. And teasing you?" A low, wicked laugh follows. "That's my new drug of choice."

Her body tightens, every nerve alive and screaming for release. He hasn't even gotten past dinner, and already her skin feels too tight, too hot.

"I help you into the chauffeured car I ordered. As I slide in next to you, I lean over and whisper in your ear, 'It's getting more and more difficult not to touch you, Charlotte. So, I'm not going to fight it anymore.'"

The air leaves her lungs. The whisper isn't real, but *God*, it feels like it is. A shiver runs down her spine, and her hand instinctively brushes her ear, as if to wipe away the phantom touch. This might be the most erotic thing she's ever experienced—and all of it through his voice alone. The towel slips from her body as she lays back on the bed, the soft fabric forgotten as she surrenders to the pull of the fantasy.

Fingers reach up, rolling one nipple between them, and the sensation shoots straight to her clit, already swollen and desperate for attention. His words are the trigger, and her body responds like it's his hands on her, not her own. *How does he do this?*

"I moved my hand over your thigh—soft as silk, Charlotte. Fuck, the way your skin felt under my fingers... perfect." His voice drips with heat, each word drawing her further in. "As I leaned in, nipping at your ear, my hand moved slowly, savoring every inch. I didn't want to rush. We had all night, and I had the most beautiful woman in the world in my grasp, right there in the back of the sexiest car ever made."

His voice cuts through the fantasy, low and commanding. "My hand finds your already—" A deep moan escapes him, raw and filled with need. "Oh, fuck—soaked panties. My fingers slide between your folds, and—" The moan that follows nearly undoes her. Just the sound of it has her on the edge, and so far, all she's done is roll her nipples between her fingers. My fingers slid between your folds, and—"

The world around her blurs, fading into a haze of molten sensations. Each shift of her thighs against the now warm sheets sends sparks racing along her skin, as though the very fabric beneath her conspires to amplify the heat coursing through her. She can almost feel him there, his presence lingering at the edges of her awareness, tantalizingly close.

The scent of him wraps around her, heady and intoxicating, a blend of earth and fire that ignites something primal within her. It's more than a memory—it's a phantom touch that teases her senses, making her body ache for him as if he's already claimed the space beside her.

"Charlotte," he growls through the phone, "your pussy is perfect. Like my fingers were made to be buried inside you." The words, raw and full of need, make her body hum. "I slid two fingers in, slow at first, just enough to feel you, but your clit? That needed attention."

Her body responds immediately. Reaching down, two fingers rub against her clit, and it's not hard to imagine his fingers there instead, the sensation overwhelms her, every touch sending her closer to the edge, and the fantasy becomes almost too real.

"Again, I whispered in your ear, I don't think I'm going to make it to the next stop of our night without making you come, Charlotte. I hope that is ok."

Charlotte's brain suddenly yells, Hell yeah, it's ok.

"I started with a slow circular rub. Charlotte, are you following along? Are you touching yourself?"

"Yes." Charlotte says with a breath, just as she gives a tight pinch of her nipple with her left hand.

"Good, I am too," Liam says with a moan.

Holy fucking hell. She is having phone sex. This is new. Charlotte needs to be in control of every aspect of her life, so allowing someone to have any type of control over her, especially when she can't even see their face, would never happen, at least not until tonight. No, she needs to be honest. It's all Liam. This man makes her feel safe enough to let him have her. She'll worry about how scary that is another time.

Liam cuts into her thoughts. "I then slid your sexy as fuck dress down to expose your perfect nipples. Damn woman. Thank you for not wearing a bra. That was the best present I have ever received." Liam says with a sexy smile. She can hear it. "You clearly liked it when I sucked hard. Your back arched, and your head dropped back giving me a better angle at your entire body. Charlotte, are you arching your back now?"

"Fuck yeah." And Charlotte arches and rubs her clit with a new intensity.

"Good." He says and goes back to the story. "You were getting close, so I sped up the rubbing and pushed down ever so slightly to give you the extra pressure you needed. I let go of your nipple and once again whispered in your ear, come for me, Charlotte."

Charlotte grits Liam's name through clenched teeth, every muscle in her body strung tight as she obeys his command. The release that follows is overwhelming— waves of pleasure crashing through her, unraveling every ounce of tension until she feels weightless. The orgasm floods her body, leaving her trembling, breathless, like she's floating in a haze of warmth and light. Her limbs feel loose, boneless, but even through the haze, a flicker of curiosity stirs. Her voice, soft and spent, breaks the quiet. "Did you...?"

There's a pause, a beat of silence where the intimacy of the moment settles between them, and then his voice, deep and soothing, answers. "You don't worry about me. This was all about you." His tone is steady but teasing. "Besides, there's still an act two."

Her breath catches in her throat, the idea sending

another ripple of heat through her already sensitive body. "Oh, shit," she whispers, still coming down from the high, her chest rising and falling with each deep breath.

Liam's voice softens, shifting back to the shy, familiar tone she's grown to know. "Thank you for sharing that with me, Charlotte. It was beautiful."

The sincerity in his words catches her off guard, and suddenly, she feels vulnerable in a way she didn't expect. Shyness creeps in, warmth spreading across her cheeks as she gathers herself. "That was... incredible, Liam." Her voice is softer now, almost tentative. "Thank you for fantasizing about me."

A quiet moment passes, the connection between them palpable, even through the distance. Her body is still humming from the intensity, but now there's something more—a deep sense of closeness, of something unspoken that lingers just beneath the surface.

BITCHES, LET'S RUN

The cool night air prickles against Charlotte's skin as she steps into the clearing, the familiar pull of her wolf thrumming beneath the surface. She glances back at her pack—her sisters—each of them shedding their human forms with practiced ease.

Jade shifts first, her lean wolf shaking out a coat of russet-colored fur before darting forward, ears pricked and eager for the chase. Harper follows, her gray fur shimmering in the moonlight, steady and strong as she falls into step beside Charlotte.

Charlotte's gaze lingers on Luna, who stays rooted at the edge of the clearing. Her arms are crossed, her expression unreadable, but Charlotte doesn't need words to feel the conflict rolling off her. It hums through the pack bond—a low, steady ache, like a wound that refuses to heal.

"You go," Luna says, her voice firm, but her gaze flickers to the forest, betraying a moment of longing. "Someone has to keep watch."

Charlotte's wolf bristles, uneasy with Luna staying behind yet again. She feels the frustration rise, hot and sharp, but she swallows it down. Luna's beasts are hers to manage, her secrets to keep, and Charlotte won't force her. Not yet.

"Thank you," Charlotte says, her voice softer than she intends. It's not just gratitude for Luna's excuse—it's for her presence. Even when Luna doesn't run, she stays close. Always close.

Turning back to the pack, Charlotte lets her wolf rise. The shift is seamless, her black fur blending into the shadows as she steps forward, taking her place at the head of the group. Her wolf's instincts sharpen, the bond with her pack humming like a live wire.

Without a word, they move as one, paws pounding against the earth in perfect rhythm. The forest comes alive around them—branches swaying in the breeze, the rustle of leaves underfoot, the distant howl of coyotes who know better than to cross their path.

Jade races ahead, darting between trees, her energy boundless. Harper stays close to Charlotte's flank, steady and unshakable. They run together, their movements synchronized, the thrill of the hunt coursing through their veins even without prey to chase.

But the absence of Luna's wolf prickles at Charlotte, gnawing at the edges of her focus. Her wolf feels it too, the gap in the bond that should be whole. Luna's presence still presses against her senses—a quiet pulse at the edge of the clearing—but it's not the same.

From her peripheral vision, Charlotte catches Luna watching, her arms wrapped tightly around herself. The sight tugs at something deep within her—a mix of pride and frustration. Luna is part of the pack, even like this, but the tension of her withheld beasts ripples through them all.

One day, Charlotte thinks, they'll run together. Fully. Freely. But that day isn't today.

Shaking off the thought, Charlotte howls, her voice rising into the night, carrying across the hills. Jade and Harper join in, their voices melding into a song of freedom and power.

This is who they are—wild, strong, unstoppable. A force no one can break. And even from the sidelines, Charlotte feels Luna, tethered to them as surely as if she ran beside them.

IT'S AN ICE CREAM
KIND OF MORNING

The next morning, Charlotte steps into the kitchen, catching sight of Luna and Jade at the oversized round table in the dining room. Out of the corner of her eye, she notices Jade cutting into a pancake the size of a frisbee.

"Hey Alpha, we've decided we like the round table," Jade announces, her tone half-serious, half-playful.

"Yeah? I only chose it so you and Ludicrous Luna over there wouldn't fight over who's more important and should sit at the head." Charlotte hadn't thought any of them would actually use it. The designer claimed the space "needed filling", so round it became. "Morning, ladies," Charlotte adds with a grin.

Jade eyes her with curiosity. "Okay, who is he, and can I get his number? If he can make you smile like that before coffee, he must be a god amongst men."

A wave of possessiveness rolls through Charlotte, unexpected and fierce. "No," she growls, the word slipping out without permission.

Luna and Jade exchange a look—*what the fuck?*—then turn back to Charlotte, eyebrows raised.

"He's not here anymore. He was just passing through." Charlotte waves off the tension, steering the conversation elsewhere. "So, Luna, good call on finding Isabell. She's amazing."

Charlotte catches Luna still watching her, suspicion flickering in her gaze before she shifts gears. "Yeah, Jade and I were just talking about her. She told us we had to sit at the table if we wanted her food." Luna adopts Isabell's no-nonsense Mexican accent. "'Beautiful table go to waste. You sit there, and I feed. No sit there? No feed.'" Luna switches back to her normal voice, smirking. "And by golly, I'm sitting here if that's all it takes to get her food. It's the best shit I've eaten in years."

Jade snorts. "Just don't let Harper hear you say that."

Luna shoots a quick glance over her shoulder, mock panic flashing across her face. "Oh shit, please don't tell Harper I said that."

Charlotte chuckles, shaking her head. "So, you didn't decide you liked the table because of the table. Food motivation goes a long way, huh?"

Luna smirks, shrugging unapologetically. "Hey, Isabell's food could make me love a rock if I had to sit on it to eat."

Charlotte grins and turns toward the kitchen, only to nearly collide with Isabell, who appears like clockwork, carrying a tray piled with Charlotte's favorites—scrambled eggs with feta, spinach, mushrooms, and a steaming cup of coffee with her favorite creamer.

"Wow, Isabell! How did you know exactly what I wanted this morning?"

Isabell shrugs, her expression unreadable but warm. "I just know," she says matter-of-factly, setting the tray down in front of a empty chair with the kind of efficiency that makes her indispensable.

At just four-foot-eight, Isabell's small frame is packed with enough sass and presence to fill the entire house. She moved into the staff quarters three days ago, and it already feels like the place revolves around her. The ladies adore her. Isabell runs the house with an iron hand, keeping them all in line, well-fed, and somehow managing to know what they need before they do.

Charlotte takes a seat, savoring the first sip of coffee as her mind drifts back to last night's call. After one of the most sensual experiences of her life, Liam had slipped into stories that made her laugh—stories about a she-wolf in Alberta who wouldn't leave him alone, even stalking him from a purple bush outside his hotel room. She had laughed harder than she had in a long time, enjoying how easy it was to listen to him. He hadn't asked for anything in return, hadn't pushed her to share her own stories.

"They talked—or rather, Liam talked—for another hour. His stories made her laugh, the kind of laugh she hadn't felt in years, and when he asked—gently, without presumption —if he could call again tonight, it caught her off guard. No one had ever asked her what she wanted. Not like that. The thought lingered, its warmth as unfamiliar as it was intoxicating."

Lost in thought, she barely notices Jade and Luna staring at her until she snaps back to the present. "What?" she asks, looking from one to the other.

"Holy tits, Char. You like a boy," Luna says, beaming like she's discovered some great secret.

"Stop, Luna," Charlotte tries to sound firm, but the small smile pokes through anyway.

"Oh, *fuck me!*" Jade's eyes widen with shock. "No damn

way. We thought *Harper* would be the one to bring a male into the pack, not you."

"What? Why would Harper bring a man into the pack?"

Another look passes between Jade and Luna before Jade speaks up. "You didn't see the way she and that Lucas guy were eyeing each other at Crimson Moon? Luna and I think she's already met him."

"No, I didn't see that! I was kind of busy trying to focus on the story that's supposed to save our pack and, you know, getting proposed to. My mind wasn't exactly on Harper's puppy lust," Charlotte snaps, frustration bubbling up.

Luna's voice turns playful. "Sorry to be the bearer of bad news, then. Harper has a boy, too."

"There is no *too*," Charlotte says, trying to hold onto control. "There's no boy for me. I had a nice time with a male last night, but that's where it will end."

Jade's eyebrows shoot up. "Oh, balls. You said 'male,' so it's a shifter, not a human. And what do you mean *will* end? If he's gone, why hasn't it already ended?"

Charlotte can feel herself backing into a corner. Then she notices the realization dawning in Jade's eyes, like a lightbulb switching on. Keeping her poker face intact, Charlotte thinks, *Oh shit, this is about to get messy.*

"Are you for real, Alpha? It's the guy from the gym. The one who took down Dylan. I cleaned up his mess!" Jade's voice rises, her face turning a shade of red that Charlotte rarely sees.

"Yes, his name is Liam. We ran into each other. I at least owed him a beer," Charlotte tries to justify, the words feeling hollow as they leave her mouth.

"But you were home last night, Alpha. So, when exactly did these beers happen?"

Shit on a biscuit. Jade's too sharp for her own good. Charlotte takes a slow sip of her coffee, trying to buy herself a moment. "We went out the other night," she says, keeping her tone casual. "Then we talked on the phone for a bit last night. He's left the state now."

"Wait. What? You *talked* on the phone? You gave your number to a shifter male?" Luna beams, a huge smile spreading across her face.

"Char, I am *so* proud of you. Hold please." With that, Luna darts out of the room.

Charlotte takes a bite of her eggs and glances at Jade. "What are we holding for?"

Jade shrugs, smirking. "It's Luna. Who the fuck knows?"

Moments later, Luna skips back into the room, juggling three pints of ice cream. She hands Jade a pint of Mint Chocolate Chip Cookie, passes Charlotte the Chocolate Chip Cookie Dough, and plops down with her own pint.

"You realize it's 8:30 in the morning?" Jade quirks an eyebrow as she examines her pint.

"Sooooo. We're motherfucking she-wolves, and we can eat ice cream at whatever time we deem necessary. And since we're about to get the dirt on our new Alpha Daddy, I say ice cream is *necessary*," Luna declares, digging into her pint with enthusiasm.

Jade just shrugs and cracks open the lid.

"No, he is not your new Alpha 'Daddy,'" Charlotte's voice cuts through the air with just a hint of power, and both Luna and Jade instinctively flinch, folding in on themselves.

Jade rubs her temples, wincing. "Damn, Alpha. Was that necessary?"

Charlotte scrunches her nose, the power surge already fading. "Sorry, ladies. Didn't mean to push any of that on you." She exhales, trying to shake off the frustration. "I just need to make it clear. I enjoyed his company more than most, but he's a lone wolf, just passing through. He's already in Arizona, heading east." With that, she pushes the plate forward and scoops a hefty bite of ice cream, the cold dessert helping to cool the heat simmering beneath her skin. Luna was right—ice cream was a good call.

Luna side-eyes Jade, lowering her voice like they're about to dive into something scandalous. "Okay. No more giving you a hard time. But seriously, what's different about him? Is he cute?"

Charlotte can't stop the grin that spreads across her face. Her defenses are crumbling, and part of her isn't even trying to stop it. "He's hot as fucking hell, but he doesn't even know it. He's just this big ol' nerd who loves rocks. Sent me a picture of him in front of the Grand Canyon. You want to see him?"

Luna's eyebrows wiggle, mischief dancing in her eyes. "Umm, do dogs lick their balls?"

"Ew, Luna." Jade scrunches her face, clearly unimpressed with the imagery.

Charlotte pulls up the picture, one she's saved and pulled up at least thirty times since last night, and hands the phone to Jade first.

As Jade and Luna lean in, scrutinizing the picture, Charlotte feels a pull deep inside—something she hadn't planned for, something she's been trying to ignore. She's realizing her feelings run deeper than she wanted to admit, and damn if the timing could be any worse. There's a reason he's a lone wolf. He didn't share the full story, but it's clear he's walking his own path, haunted by his own demons.

Her jaw tightens as the weight of it all presses down. She can't drag him into the mess that is the Red Rocks right now. The pack's problems are too dangerous, too messy, and his life? His life is more important than her feelings. When he calls, she'll have to tell him staying in touch isn't a good idea. She'll let him go. She has to. Even if it feels like tearing something vital away.

Jade hands the phone back, eyebrows raised in a way that makes Charlotte's skin prickle. "Okay, yeah, he's definitely not what I expected. Hot nerds are dangerous."

"Agreed," Luna chimes in, her eyes still glued to the screen like she's committing every detail to memory. "A nerd who looks like that? Char, you might be in trouble."

Charlotte forces a laugh, hoping it sounds convincing, but her wolf shifts uneasily beneath the surface. The instinct to protect, to hold on, wars with the ironclad truth she keeps repeating to herself: letting him go is the only choice. Her pack comes first. It always has. It always will.

But even as the thought settles, the echo of his voice lingers, tugging at her in ways she doesn't want to name. The idea of hearing it one more time clings to her, soft and insistent, like the whisper of a storm rolling in from the distance—beautiful and dangerous, impossible to ignore

MADDY

Liam closes the app after booking a mule ride to the bottom of the canyon. The irony isn't lost on him —a wolf riding a mule. He smirks, already crafting a joke to toss at Charlotte when he calls her tonight. Reaching into the back of the Bronco for his day pack, his phone chimes.

Swiping the screen, he sees a text from Brian:

> Hey, man. I think Maddy's in trouble.

A cold rush hits Liam's gut. Instantly, his thumb slams the video call button. The screen flickers to life, and Brian's face appears, his brow furrowed with concern.

"What do you mean, Maddy might be in trouble?" The words come out sharper than intended, but Liam's nerves are already coiled.

Brian shakes his head. "Stacy's been trying to get ahold of her for over a week. She finally called Leo, and he said Maddy was out at the store. But something didn't sit right.

Liam's jaw tightens. Maddy. His kid sister. The Gold

Beach Pack—his old pack—still clings to the old laws, and while Brian's been working to change that as Alpha, it was too late for Maddy. She'd been promised to Leo years ago, bound to a mate she didn't choose.

"She's gone quiet before," Brian continues, his voice hesitant, "but never this long. A day or two, maybe three— but a whole week? My gut is kicking up, something isn't right man.

Liam exhales slowly, his fingers gripping the edge of the Bronco's window. "Maddy will take my throat if I show up ready to kill that bastard and it turns out she's just taking a girls' weekend." The words are light, but his wolf doesn't buy it, and neither does Brian.

"Maybe," Brian replies, though doubt flickers in his voice. "But I've got an enforcer headed to Gold Beach now to get eyes on her. I'll know more by morning."

Liam exhales, tension thick in his chest. "Alright. Keep me posted. I'll head north tomorrow, but I'll wait to hear what your enforcer finds out before I charge in blind."

Brian nods, his shoulders slumping a little. "Good call.

A small grin cracks through Brian's serious expression. "Also, Stacy's losing her shit. She shifted this morning and came at me like I was the damn enemy. I'm hobbling around waiting for my thigh to heal because she couldn't keep her claws to herself. You might want to get up here sooner rather than later and be her new punching bag. She's got big badger energy, and it's all aimed at me right now."

Liam snorts despite himself. "She's feisty. Better you than me, Bro."

Brian sobers, his tone softening. "Seriously, though. Be careful, Liam. And call me before you leave."

The line goes dead, and Liam leans back against the Bronco, his mind racing. He trusts Brian's instincts, but this feels different. Maddy might disappear for a day or two, but a week? That's not like her. Still, it doesn't sound like immediate danger—not yet. He needs to keep his head clear for whatever comes next.

The drive takes him as far as the Nevada state line before exhaustion sets in. His wolf growls in frustration, but Liam knows better than to push through the night. He spots a motel sign a few miles out and lets out a sigh. One night. That's all. He'll rest, check in with Brian in the morning.

As he pulls off the highway, a thought tugs at him— Vegas is less than an hour away. If he's stopping anyway, why not check in with Charlotte? Her sharp wit and steady presence might be the only thing to cut through the chaos in his head.

It's just for a few hours, he tells himself. A drink, maybe a laugh. Then back on the road.

TRUTHS ARE SCARY

After downing half a pint of ice cream and blabbing with the girls about her nerdy wolf, Charlotte heads to the gym. The familiar clank of weights and hum of machines fill the air as she strolls the floor, greeting members and casually stepping in to stop Ralph from hulking out on a deadlift that's clearly too much for him.

"Easy there, Superman," she says, raising an eyebrow. "We don't need to call an ambulance today."

Ralph grins sheepishly, backing off the bar. Satisfied, Charlotte moves on, shaking her head at the near-disaster.

By the time she settles into her office, the adrenaline from the floor has leveled out, leaving her with just enough quiet to think. Too much quiet. Her phone buzzes, breaking the silence, and a small smile tugs at the corner of her mouth when she sees the message.

> Hey gorgeous. I'll be in Vegas tonight. Can I take you to dinner?

I thought you were heading east?

She fires back, a slight frown creasing her brow.

> I have to make my way back to Oregon.
> Family stuff. I'll tell you tonight, but only
> after food.

Charlotte exhales, the weight of the decision pressing on her chest. *Is this a good idea?* Her thumb hovers over the keyboard before she types:

> Call me when you get to town. I'll meet you.

The second she hits send, her heart thuds a little faster. Jase's voice rings in her head, as clear as if he were standing behind her: *Really? You let a lone wolf back into your territory? I didn't get the memo that hell froze over.*

She shakes her head, brushing the thought aside. It's just dinner. Nothing more.

Her phone buzzes again, pulling her out of her spiraling thoughts. This time, it's from Harper:

> Hey Char. Lunch? I'm testing a new special
> and need a Guinea Pig.

> Yeah, what's for lunch?

She types back without hesitation, knowing full well it'll be delicious.

> You know me. It's all about the cheese.

Harper, Executive Chef at the most exclusive spot on the strip, never disappoints when it comes to food.

AN HOUR LATER, Charlotte finds herself seated at *X'tase,* an impossibly elegant restaurant that caters to the rich and famous. It's almost surreal, like stepping into a world where everything sparkles. She sinks into a velvet booth, the deep purple fabric soft against her skin. Above her, crystal chandeliers of varying sizes dangle from the ceiling, casting a soft glow. The whole place feels like royalty could walk in at any moment.

How did I get here? she wonders. Crawling through the mud to escape her past feels like a lifetime ago, and yet, here she sits in opulence.

"Hey, Char." Harper's voice reaches her before she even needs to look. Charlotte senses her approach without effort —the same way she always does. Harper slides into the seat across from her, that familiar calm confidence intact, a presence Charlotte has leaned on more times than she can count.

"Thanks for the invite. I haven't been here since opening

night. Forgot how over-the-top this place is," Charlotte says, glancing around at the luxury surrounding them.

Harper grins, the edges of her smile tugging at something in Charlotte's chest. "Yeah, it's a bit over the top. The General Manager's cool, though. She lets me get wild with my pairings. Remember back in Black Canyon when I used apple sauce instead of mayo on the chicken sandwiches? People thought I'd lost my mind until I got Jade to try it. Then it blew up."

Charlotte smirks, the memory hitting with a rush of warmth. "Oh, I remember. I think they were ready to kick us out of the territory for shaking things up too much. But we got so damn good at fighting, they decided to tolerate the crazy."

Harper chuckles, shaking her head. "The pack chef hated me after that. Can't help it if my food was better."

Taking a sip of iced tea, Charlotte watches her friend— the woman who has stood beside her through every storm. There's a bond here, one deeper than words. "So... what's up?" The words come out casually, but Charlotte knows Harper too well. She feels the shift in the air, the weight Harper's carrying.

Harper shifts slightly, her confidence faltering for a moment. "Why do you think something's up, Alpha?"

Charlotte arches an eyebrow, amusement flickering at the corners of her lips. "For one, you've never invited me to lunch. It's felt like you've been avoiding me lately. And now, you're calling me Alpha. That's a giveaway."

Harper stumbles for a reply, her voice coming out too quickly. "I call you Alpha all the time."

Charlotte scoffs, gently, "No. Jade calls me Alpha. You don't." Leaning forward slightly, her eyes soften. "So, I'll ask again. What's up?"

Harper exhales, the weight of whatever's on her mind finally slipping through. "Fine. I've been thinking about the Redwood Alpha's offer."

Charlotte feels the shift, the real question hanging in the air. She hadn't given Spencer's offer much thought today—Liam's impending return has distracted her, offered a reprieve from the endless cycle of overthinking. "I don't know," she admits, her voice quieter than she intended. "I'd do anything for the safety of this pack. But... I don't know if this makes sense."

Harper doesn't interrupt, giving Charlotte space to wrestle with her thoughts.

"What assurances do I have that the Redwoods will actually keep the Red Rocks safe? And we didn't even talk about living arrangements. What, I'm supposed to live in California? That leaves you, Luna, and Jade without an Alpha." Charlotte shakes her head. "That won't work."

"We need to hash it out," she says firmly, the weight of leadership pressing down harder. "Let's come up with the questions we need answers to, then I'll call Spencer."

"That's fair. It was a shock," Harper agrees, signing an invoice that's been brought to her without breaking stride. "You know you have my fealty, Alpha. Whatever decision you make, I'll support it. But... I think getting a strong ally is a good idea."

Charlotte leans back, staring at her for a beat longer than necessary. Harper's words aren't just empty loyalty—they're backed by action, by years of standing shoulder to shoulder in the most dangerous moments. "You might be right, but we don't know enough about them. We need to investigate before I agree to something that's more than an alliance—it's a fucking wedding. We've got a hacker in our pack. Shouldn't we use that skill before binding me to someone I don't even know?"

The memories flicker across Charlotte's mind like ghosts —memories of a future she fought to escape. Her hand lifts to her throat, fingers grazing her collarbone. "I thought I got away from this."

Harper watches her carefully, the tension between them thick but familiar. Harper has always been the one who sees Charlotte's cracks, the one who knows the parts of her no one else can.

"I get the feeling this is a good pack," Harper says softly, her eyes lowering to the drink between her hands. She rubs the condensation on the glass with her thumbs, her movements thoughtful.

Before Charlotte can dig deeper, a bowl is placed in front of her. She takes a bite, her mind instantly hijacked by the taste. Harper knows her shit, and Charlotte isn't shy about admitting it. "I'm sorry, Harp. I didn't hear a fucking word you just said. I'm too busy enjoying heaven in a bowl."

Harper's chin tips up slightly, pride flickering in her eyes. "Thanks, Char." She takes her own bite and groans. "Damn, you're right. This is good." She doesn't even pause, speaking through a mouthful. "So I heard you've got a hot nerd beefcake you're hiding from us."

Charlotte lifts her eyes, a smirk creeping across her face. "Funny. I hear the same about you."

Harper's eyes widen in surprise, mirroring Charlotte's earlier reaction. For a moment, they just stare at each other, the silence stretching before simultaneous smiles break through.

"Okay, so apparently, there are no secrets in this pack. Who figured it out—Jade, because she's suspicious of everything? Or Luna, because... well, she's Luna?"

Charlotte shrugs. "No idea. They let it slip this morning. Said you and Lucas were making googly eyes at the meeting."

Harper's eyes widen again, realization dawning. "Ooookay. Guess it's my turn." Her voice softens. "Lucas Williams, Redwood Pack."

Charlotte meets her gaze, the protective instinct kicking in. "I know who he is."

"I think he's my mate, Char."

Confusion crosses Charlotte's face, but she can't hide it fast enough. Harper's vulnerability is rare, and the suspicion in Charlotte's eyes tells all.

"I can't get him out of my mind. When we ran into each other a couple months ago—" Charlotte's mind screams, *a couple months?!* "—I thought it was just attraction. We hooked up, and it was... fireworks."

Harper looks down at her glass, her voice softer than usual. "It hasn't stopped. I want him every day. I've never felt this before, except with that one guy, Doug. But that was just because he was... *talented*." She smirks. "Lucas? He's different. I'd burn the world for him. His touch is a drug, Char. I want his scent all over me. I know it sounds gross, but... it's the truth."

Charlotte understands more than she wants to admit. Harper's words mirror her own unspoken thoughts about Liam, but she can't voice them. Not yet.

"Okay, Harper. I hear you." Charlotte's voice softens, trying to convey the compassion Harper needs.

Harper looks up, searching Charlotte's face.

"You're scared," Charlotte says, reading her expression.

"Yeah. I am," Harper admits, her voice shaking. "This will change everything."

The truth hits like a punch to the gut. Everything *will*

change. The pack is standing at a crossroads, and every choice leads to a different future. The fear of those unknown paths twists in Charlotte's gut, but she won't let fear drive her decisions. Not now. Not ever.

"Harper, no matter what we do, change is inevitable. What matters is how we decide to face it. It's up to us whether the change makes us sad, anxious, or... happy. And remember," Charlotte lowers her head, catching Harper's eyes. "If the decision isn't right, we can always make another one."

As the words leave her mouth, Charlotte isn't sure who they're meant for—Harper, or herself.

They finish lunch, strolling together toward the parking lot. The conversation flows easily, their bond a constant undercurrent. As they walk, Charlotte feels the weight of her own emotions bubbling up—the excitement she's been trying to push down.

"Okay, so," Charlotte starts, a grin pulling at the corner of her lips. "Liam's coming back tonight."

Harper glances sideways, a knowing smile already forming. "Ah, the hot nerd returns. You excited?"

Charlotte can't hold back the smirk. "Yeah. I didn't expect it, but I am." She laughs softly, the sound surprising even to her own ears. *When the hell did I start laughing and smiling like this?* The woman who used to be tough as nails, unshakeable, now catches herself smiling and giggling over a guy. *What the fuck is that?*

"I don't know what it is about him," Charlotte continues, shaking her head slightly, almost in disbelief. "But I've never felt this." Her tone softens, a vulnerability slipping through that she usually keeps locked away.

Harper watches her carefully, that knowing look in her

eyes. "Yeah? How excited?" She raises her eyebrow, teasing but genuine.

Charlotte hesitates for a moment, but this is Harper. If there's anyone she can open up to, it's her. "Let's just say... we've been doing some phone play."

Harper's eyes widen in mock shock. "Phone play? Charlotte Randolph?" She lets out a teasing laugh. "Girl, I'm going to need details. What exactly does 'phone play' with a hot wolf nerd look like?"

Charlotte's cheeks flush slightly, but the grin stays on her face. "It started pretty tame, you know? A few flirty texts. But last night..."

"Last night?" Harper prompts, leaning in like they're two teenagers gossiping about their crushes.

"Well, let's just say Liam's got a way with words," Charlotte admits, feeling the heat rise again just thinking about it. "He was painting a picture, telling me exactly what he did to me in his fantasy, and... damn. He wasn't even with me, and I still nearly came apart."

Harper lets out a low whistle. "Damn, Char. Didn't know nerds could be so... talented."

"Oh, believe me, I was just as surprised. But, it's more than that. It's like... he gets me. I've never been this open with someone before, especially not this fast. It feels... natural."

Harper nods, her teasing fading into something more thoughtful. "Sounds like he's already gotten under your skin, Char. And I think that scares the hell out of you."

Charlotte sighs, glancing at Harper with a small smile. "Yeah, it does." The admission weighs heavier than it should. Beneath the excitement, there's something else gnawing at her, something she can't shake. *Am I going soft?* The thought makes her stomach twist. She's never been the type to let anyone close enough to get inside her head like this. *I can't afford to be weak now. Not with everything that's coming.* Her pack needs her strong, unbreakable.

She looks away for a moment, the weight of what she knows she has to do pressing down on her chest. "I'm excited to see him tonight, but... I think I need to end things."

Harper tilts her head, concern creasing her brow. "End things? What do you mean?"

Charlotte takes a breath, her voice lowering. "I'm afraid he's making me weak, Harp. I'm catching myself smiling and laughing—hell, *giggling*—and it's like... I'm losing my edge. I can't afford to be soft right now. I need my strength for the fight that's coming."

Harper frowns, her gaze sharpening. "Soft? Char, you're the strongest person I know. Having feelings for someone doesn't make you weak. If anything, it makes you more powerful—if you let it."

"I don't know," Charlotte admits, running a hand through her hair. "I just... I can't let my guard down. Not now. My wolf's calm around him, and I don't know what to make of that. It's like she's already accepted him. But I can't. Not with everything at stake."

Harper's voice softens, but there's an edge of firmness to it. "Your wolf trusts him, Char. That's not something to ignore. But if you really think cutting things off is the right move... just make sure it's not fear talking."

Charlotte exhales, the inner battle raging inside her. "Maybe. But tonight, I need to tell him. I need to focus on the pack. I can't let anything weaken me right now."

Harper bumps her shoulder lightly. "You deserve to feel something besides vigilant and guarded, Char."

As they reach the parking lot, Charlotte feels lighter, the

weight of her internal struggle a little less suffocating. Harper's presence always has that effect—grounding her, reminding her that she doesn't have to carry everything alone.

"Thanks, Harp," Charlotte says, sincerity filling her voice. "For everything."

Harper smiles softly, her eyes warm. "Always, Char. You know I've got your back."

They stop at their cars, and Charlotte feels a wave of affection for the woman standing beside her. Years ago, Harper had saved her—literally, more than once—and now, emotionally, she's still the one holding Charlotte steady.

"You know, I'm glad you told me about Lucas," Charlotte adds, giving Harper a playful nudge. "If you think he's your mate, we probably have to have some conversations with the other ladies."

Harper laughs, a genuine sound that softens the tension between them. "Maybe. But you better protect me from Jade."

"Deal." Charlotte grins, feeling a flicker of excitement, but it's quickly swallowed by the heaviness pressing on her chest. The excitement is there, but it's tangled with sadness, a weight she can't shake. *I can't give in.* For the first time in a long while, she wants to let herself feel something more, but tonight... tonight she knows she has to let it go. Liam will be back, and maybe things could change if she let them. But she can't afford that. Not now.

As much as she craves the connection, the reality pulls her back. *I need to be strong. I can't let myself go soft.* The pack needs her focused, sharp, and unshakable for the battle ahead. There's no room for distractions, no matter how much her heart pulls toward him.

They part with easy smiles, and Charlotte heads to her

truck. The familiar hum of the engine settles her, though it does little to quiet the anticipation buzzing beneath her skin —a tangled mix of excitement and anxiety.

As she drives, her thoughts drift to Liam—his voice, the warmth in his words that lingers long after their calls. Her chest tightens. She knows she should cut things off tonight. The pack comes first; it always has. *I can't afford distractions. Not now.*

But the thought of shutting Liam out tugs at her heart in a way she didn't expect. Her wolf stirs, whispering a word she's not ready to hear: *Mate.*

The instinct is undeniable, sending a shiver down her spine. She grips the steering wheel tighter, trying to push it away. *No. I can't let this happen. I need to stay strong.*

Her wolf doesn't resist. It doesn't argue. It simply waits— calm and certain, like it already knows the truth she's too afraid to admit. Liam is the one.

Charlotte shakes her head, trying to smother the pull. But no matter how hard she fights, the thought of him keeps slipping through, warming the cracks she's fought so hard to seal.

Fear twists in her chest, but so does something else—a flicker of excitement, dangerous and real. For the first time in a long while, she lets herself feel it, even if only for a moment.

DONKEY KONG

After what feels like three days but is really only a few hours, Charlotte hears the cosmic, futuristic ringtone she set for Liam's profile. It's reminds her of the stupid shirt he wore the day they met. She taps the answer button. "Hey there. Did you make it to Vegas?"

"Just pulled into town," Liam's voice comes through, warm and a little excited. "I thought I'd call and see where you want to meet? I'll figure out a hotel from there."

Before her brain can intervene, her mouth is already moving. "Don't do that. You can crash in one of the spare rooms."

Silence on the other end. Then, "Really? That would be awesome. Saves some cash."

Charlotte blinks, stunned that those words fell out so easily. "Oh... okay. I'll send you the pin on Maps. See you soon." She hangs up, staring at her phone. *What the hell was that?* She hadn't planned to make that offer, but now it's out there. "Isabell!"

As if summoned by magic, Isabell appears from nowhere. "Si, Miss Charlotte?"

"Holy shit! How do you do that?" Charlotte's a damn wolf shifter, with bloodlines straight from the first of her kind. Enhanced hearing and sight are just two of her super-powers, yet this tiny four-foot-nothing firecracker manages to sneak up on her every time.

Once she catches her breath, Charlotte asks, "Which room is ready for a guest?"

Isabell's response is simple, "Oh, any of them, señora." With that, she turns on her heel and vanishes as quickly as she appeared. Charlotte wonders, *How did we ever live without her?*

After checking the room farthest from her own—because keeping some distance feels necessary—Charlotte sinks into the massive sectional, flipping on the ridiculously large TV. On-screen, a character tosses out a sarcastic quip to his friend—they're clearly both scientists—and she laughs, suddenly realizing: it all makes sense now. *I have a thing for nerds.*

The doorbell chimes, echoing through the house, and Charlotte jumps slightly. "Speak of the devil," she mutters under her breath. Trying to keep a casual pace, her wolf is grinning wide inside her. *Fine,* she concedes. *We'll have fun tonight, but he can't stay.*

In the foyer, Charlotte thanks Isabell for answering the door and finds Liam standing there, wide-eyed, soaking in the grandeur of the house. His mouth hangs open, a mix of awe and disbelief written across his face.

Charlotte grins, feeling an odd sense of pride. Impressing him feels good in a way she wasn't expecting. "I should've warned you. It's slightly pretentious."

Liam's eyes roam the space, from the dark European oak staircases to the black gothic-inspired chandelier that dangles dramatically from the third floor like something straight out of a Dracula movie. "Holy macaroni, Charlotte! This place is insane." His enthusiasm is palpable, and Charlotte can't help but laugh. His nerdy charm is so damn endearing.

"I know. It took my breath away the first time too." She gestures around. "So, tour and then dinner? Or dinner, then tour? The place is kind of small, so it won't take long."

Before Liam can answer, Isabell appears like a rabbit from a hat, speaking up from behind. "Give ten minutes for dinner." And just as quickly, she's gone.

Charlotte jumps, turning to where Isabell had stood. "We were going to go out, Isabell! You don't have to worry about us!"

Isabell's head peeks out from the doorway. "Ni se te ocurra," she mutters, then disappears again. Charlotte sighs. "So... tour it is, I guess."

Liam snickers, his amusement shining through. "Is she always like that?"

"Like what? An unstoppable force? Yes." Charlotte shakes her head, a smirk tugging at her lips. "I swear she can teleport."

They start the tour, and Liam's eyes light up with every detail—the intricate woodwork, the opulence of the chandelier, the sweeping staircases. "I feel like I just walked into a *Dungeons & Dragons* castle. Seriously, if there's a secret trapdoor or hidden scroll somewhere, let me know." His grin is infectious, and Charlotte finds herself giggling again.

She's never been one to laugh this much around anyone, but there's something about Liam's presence that brings it out of her. It's easy. Comfortable. But her wolf's quiet approval hums under her skin, reminding her that this is more than just attraction. There's a pull—a connection she's not ready to name.

As they round the corner, Liam glances at her, his grin widening. "This place is massive. You sure you're not hiding a secret lair or something?"

Charlotte laughs, shaking her head. "No secret lairs, sorry. Just... a lot of rooms we hardly ever use."

Liam shrugs, his easy charm on full display. "Shame. I was hoping for something out of a spy movie."

"Of course you were," Charlotte says, rolling her eyes with a smirk.

Liam is still trying to soak it all in as they head up the stairs, his eyes wide as they pass more grand features of the house. "Isabell put you in the open Master bedroom so you could have your own space," Charlotte explains as they reach the third floor. She opens the last door on the right, but as the door swings open, her face flushes. "Oh shit! Wrong door." She's a bit embarrassed that she's still learning her way around her own house and really just how many linen closets this house has. "Let's try this one."

Finally, she opens the correct door. Liam steps inside, and his expression transforms. The room is modern but masculine, with clean lines and dark tones. A sitting area by the window frames a perfect view of the lake. But Charlotte's eyes can't help but drift toward the bed, which sticks out with its fluffy black and teal comforter, decorated with what feels like way too many pillows. *That bed needs quality testing,* she thinks, a flush creeping up her neck at the thought.

"Will this work?" she asks, trying to play it cool. But the question hangs heavier than it should. *Why does his approval mean so much?*

Liam looks like a kid in a candy store. "Fuck yeah, this will work. This is crazy, Charlotte." His voice echoes slightly as he disappears into the bathroom. "Holy schnikies! The tub is bigger than my living room back home!"

Charlotte can't help but smile. Her wolf stays calm, unusually so, even with a man in their den. *Why is she so quiet? We can't keep him,* Charlotte reminds herself, but her wolf doesn't seem to care, practically curled up in contentment.

When Liam is done marveling over the bathroom, they continue the tour. His amazement at the house is downright adorable. Charlotte saves the game room for last, knowing that Luna and Jade are lying in wait, like wolves about to pounce. Liam slows his steps as they near the doorway, his instincts sharp. "This is the Rukus Room," Charlotte introduces, just as they step inside the expansive space.

Liam senses the energy in the room, his posture tightening as he approaches the threshold cautiously. *Smart wolf.* "Liam, these are my packmates, Luna and Jade."

Both women stand and offer their hands in acknowledgment. Jade smirks, her eyes sharp. "Nice to see you again, Liam."

"Thanks, you too," Liam replies, bowing his head slightly in respect. "It's nice to meet you both. Thanks for letting me crash in your beautiful den. This place is incredible." His gaze shifts, catching something out of the corner of his eye. "Whoa, is that Donkey Kong?" His voice rises in excitement as he sidesteps Charlotte to head straight for the old arcade machine.

Luna grins proudly. "Yep. And I have an unbeatable score."

Liam chuckles, teasing her. "Oh, I don't know. I'm pretty f'n good."

"I heard a challenge!" Luna exclaims, bouncing on her

toes with excitement. "Jade, did you hear that? He challenged me, did you hear it?"

Jade, already back at the hot-pink pool table, simply shrugs, triangle in hand. "Yeah, I heard it, Princess Pauline."

Before the challenge can escalate, Isabell appears out of nowhere. "No challenge. Dinner." Her voice cuts through the room like a command, and even Liam doesn't hesitate. Four big bad wolves, yet Isabell manages to make them all obedient in an instant. *How does she do that?* Charlotte wonders as they make their way to the dining room.

The table is loaded, and the smells are overwhelming: asada tacos, tamales, rice, beans, and all the fixings. The Lazy Susan in the center is piled high with cilantro, sour cream, chopped onions, and a mountain of Chihuahua cheese.

Luna digs in immediately. "Liam, you've got to come to dinner again next week," she mumbles between bites of enchiladas.

Charlotte stares at her, wide-eyed. *What the fuck, Luna?*

"If we get to eat like this, hell yeah!" Jade adds, her enthusiasm uncharacteristic, as a drop of cheese sauce clings to the corner of her mouth.

Charlotte notices how calm everyone seems. The tension from earlier melts into easy laughter and conversation. The air feels light for the first time in a long time.

"Don't think for a second I've forgotten about that challenge," Luna teases, pointing her fork at Liam. "Eat up, because it's on like Donkey Kong."

The banter continues as they load up their plates, just as Harper bursts into the dining room. "Holy guacamole! What smells so good?" She stops short, her eyes locking onto Liam, who is sitting in front of the pitcher of margaritas. A slow smile spreads across her face, and something in that smile brings Charlotte a sense of calm she hasn't felt in ages. For a brief moment, everything feels right.

"You must be Liam," Harper says, extending her hand. Charlotte catches the smirk tugging at Harper's lips, a silent tease that sets her on edge. "I've heard a little about you. Didn't expect to see you at our table so soon."

Liam gives a quick shake, smiling back. "You must be Harper. Thanks for letting me crash here tonight."

Harper's eyes flicker with amusement. "Of course. *Mi casa es su casa.*" She turns and calls toward the kitchen, "Did I say it right, Isabell?"

"*Sí, Miss!*" Isabell's voice calls back.

Liam chuckles, "I'm just passing through on my way back to Oregon. But thank you for the hospitality. You all have an amazing home—feels like a desert castle."

Jade's voice cuts in with her usual nonchalance. "When Alpha says something will be, it will be."

Charlotte watches Liam closely for any reaction to the word *Alpha,* but if it registers, he doesn't show it. He just keeps eating, making easy conversation with the pack, fitting in like he's always belonged. And for the first time since they moved in, Charlotte feels like the house is complete.

After dinner, Isabell shoos them out of the dining room, full and happy. Luna and Liam dive into their Donkey Kong competition, the shit-talking ramping up almost immediately. Charlotte settles on the couch, her laptop open but her attention mostly on the group. Harper and Jade start another round of 9-ball, their banter just as lively as the gaming duo's.

"You're going down, big guy," Luna declares, leaning into the joystick with fierce concentration.

Liam chuckles, relaxed but focused. "Dream on, Princess. I've been training for this moment since I was ten."

"Ten? Please," Luna scoffs. "I was breaking records before you knew how to spell Nintendo."

"Doubtful," Liam fires back, grinning. "Do they even make controllers for hands as small as yours?"

Jade cackles from across the room. "Oh, she's going to destroy you for that one. Watch out for tiny fists of fury."

"I don't need fists to win," Luna snaps, her eyes glued to the screen. "I need skill, which I have in spades. Unlike this nerd."

"'This nerd' is currently crushing your high score, so what does that say about you?" Liam's voice is all smug confidence, and it earns him an exaggerated gasp from Luna.

"Could it be?" Jade chimes in, casting a glance at the scoreboard with mock shock. "Has the great Luna finally been dethroned?"

"Noooo, what the fuck, Liam?" Luna wails, throwing her hands in the air as the words *GAME OVER* flash across her screen. She spins to face him, her expression a mix of outrage and disbelief. "I take it back! You're not invited to dinner next week."

"Hey now, you don't speak for me," Harper teases, lining up her shot at the pool table. "I'm all for someone humbling you at something."

Jade nods solemnly, chalking her cue. "Honestly, it's a public service."

"Public service?" Luna splutters, glaring at them. "I carried this pack on my back through *Mario Kart* and *Street Fighter*, and this is the thanks I get?"

"Yes," Harper says without missing a beat, sinking her shot. "You're welcome."

Everyone laughs—except Luna, who pouts dramatically, crossing her arms. "You're all traitors. I hope the Red Rocks crumble."

Charlotte shakes her head, unable to hide her smile as Liam holds up both hands in mock surrender. "Okay, okay, I'll let you win next time," he offers, though the mischievous gleam in his eyes says otherwise.

"You better," Luna grumbles, though her lips twitch as if she's fighting back a smile. "Or I'm taking your high score and your margaritas."

"You touch my margaritas, and we're throwing hands," Liam warns, his tone light but firm. "Pack or no pack."

The easy camaraderie fills the room, laughter bouncing off the walls. It's strange, Charlotte realizes, how long it's been since she's seen her pack like this—relaxed, happy, just being themselves. When was the last time we laughed like this? she wonders, a smile tugging at her lips. Their wolves have settled a bit since moving in, but they'd forgotten how to laugh, how to let go.

Harper is the first to stand, giving a wave. "I've got an early delivery of Wagyu tomorrow, so I'm out. Sleep well, everyone." She winks at Charlotte as she heads toward the door.

Jade follows soon after, dragging Luna with her under the guise of "discussing strategy for tomorrow's rematch," leaving Charlotte and Liam alone, both sitting on opposite ends of the overstuffed sectional. The distance between them feels too big, especially with the way the air thickens almost instantly, the sexual tension palpable. Charlotte shifts slightly, her body hyper-aware of his presence, while Liam leans forward, resting his elbows on his knees, as if trying to bridge the gap.

"So, why do you have to head back to Oregon?" Charlotte asks, breaking the silence.

Liam leans forward, elbows resting on his knees. "My old Alpha called. He thinks my sister might be in trouble."

Charlotte frowns. "What kind of trouble?"

Liam sighs, running a hand through his hair. "Maddy— my sister—was promised to a guy named Leo under Elder Laws. No mating bond, no love—just control. She hasn't answered her phone in a week, and something feels... off."

Charlotte inches closer, her hand brushing his thigh. "Tell me what you need."

He meets her gaze, gratitude flickering in his eyes. "You're already doing it. Being here, with you and your pack —it means more than you know." He pauses, a small, shy smile tugging at his lips. "My wolf likes you. A lot."

Charlotte's wolf stirs, humming with approval. She tilts her head, a teasing smile playing on her lips. "Think our wolves would play nice if we let them out?"

Liam's grin turns mischievous. "Oh, Charlotte, my wolf might be *too* nice."

THEIR WOLVES

Liam steps outside, the dry desert air hitting him like a wall of heat, but it doesn't bother him. His wolf paces just beneath the surface, restless, eager. Tonight isn't about pack politics or family troubles. Tonight, it's about release. About freedom. About *her*.

Charlotte's standing at the edge of the yard, her back to him, the last rays of sunlight making her black hair glow like onyx. But it's not just the human side of her that captivates him—it's her wolf. He feels it—feels her energy like a current that pulls him in.

With a deep breath, Liam lets the shift begin. Bones realign, fur pushes through skin, and in seconds, the man is gone. The black wolf that stands in his place is larger than most shifters, nearly as big as a direwolf from legends. His paws sink into the dirt as he stretches, savoring the power that surges through him in wolf form.

Charlotte turns, her own transformation swift and effortless. The moment her wolf form takes shape, Liam's breath catches. *She's beautiful.* Her black fur is sleek, glistening under the desert moon, and her build is strong, yet agile—designed for speed and cunning. She's not just fast; she's clever. The kind of wolf that wins not just through strength, but through strategy.

He can't help but watch her for a moment, taking in the way her muscles ripple under her coat, the way her eyes—sharp, glowing—lock onto his. *She's perfect,* he thinks, the admiration running deeper than he expected. She's built for this terrain, a predator at home in the desert's harsh beauty.

With a soft growl, Charlotte darts forward, her paws barely making a sound on the sandy ground. She's fast. Faster than any wolf he's run with in a long time. Liam's wolf stirs, excitement prickling his skin. *Game on.*

He takes off after her, his larger form closing the distance between them quickly. But she's clever—dipping low, twisting sharply, using the uneven terrain to her advantage. Every time he thinks he's caught up, she jukes, a flicker of motion in the dark that leaves him scrambling to adjust. A low growl of playful frustration rumbles in his throat, but he's grinning inside. *She's toying with me.*

Charlotte's wolf glances back at him, eyes flashing with mischief. *You think you can catch me?* her gaze seems to say. Liam bares his teeth in a wolfish grin, pushing harder, the powerful muscles in his legs driving him forward. She's fast, but he's got the strength, the endurance. He knows how to pace himself.

She leads him further into the desert, weaving between the scattered rocks and brush, her movements fluid and precise. It's like watching a shadow slip through the landscape, always just out of reach. But the thrill of the chase only fuels him more.

As they near a rocky outcrop, she makes a sharp turn, heading toward a steep hill. Liam picks up the pace, his breath coming in steady bursts, muscles flexing with every stride. He can feel the ground shift under his paws, the desert alive beneath him. The freedom of it is intoxicating— no boundaries, no limits. Just him and her, wild and unleashed.

Suddenly, Charlotte stops at the top of the ridge, turning to face him. Her stance is proud, her chest heaving from the run, and for a moment, they just stare at each other, both wolves breathing hard. *She's incredible.* Strong. Sleek. Fearless.

Liam's wolf slows to a halt, his gaze locked on hers. For a heartbeat, there's nothing but the sound of their panting and the quiet hum of the desert around them. But then she lets out a soft bark, a playful challenge, and takes off again, her tail wagging as she bounds down the other side of the hill.

With a burst of laughter inside, Liam follows, his larger frame moving easily now, his wolf reveling in the joy of the chase. It's not about dominance, not about winning or losing. It's about the connection—the pure, primal thrill of running together.

As they reach a wide, open stretch of desert, Charlotte slows, finally letting him catch up. When they come to a stop, side by side, the moon high above them, Liam nudges her gently with his snout, a silent gesture of affection. She responds with a nuzzle of her own, their wolves sharing a moment of quiet understanding.

She's perfect, his wolf whispers, the word sinking deep into his bones.

Liam's wolf stands taller beside her, proud, protective. He's never met a wolf quite like her. Not just because of her strength or beauty, but because of the way she moves, the way she challenges him. The way her presence quiets the storm inside him.

Together, they stand beneath the desert sky, two black wolves in the moonlight, perfectly matched.

A few hours later, with their wolves satisfied and back in human form, Charlotte and Liam walk up the stairs, the air between them thick with unspoken desire. Lust radiates like heat from a fire, drawing them closer. Liam doesn't care about fate, rules, or anything beyond getting inside this woman. This isn't about caution—caution doesn't exist in his world tonight.

Charlotte leans against a door, down the hall from his room, her hand resting on the knob. "I didn't have time to show you this room earlier," she says, her voice low, playful. "Want to see the coolest part of this house?"

Anticipation surges through him. He grins, stepping closer. "Do corgi butts wiggle?"

Her laugh—a sound she doesn't give freely—fills the hallway, and it's like music to his ears. Charlotte, the no-nonsense Alpha, laughing for him. It's a gift, one he didn't expect but treasures.

She opens the door and Liam steps into yet another impossibly luxurious room. A massive white sectional sits in a cozy nook, *The Big Bang Theory* playing on an oversized TV. His eyes roam over the space: a bed that looks like it was made for kings, linens in soft peach and white. There's a wet bar tucked into another corner, and then... "Is that an elevator?"

The mischievous look on her face sends a jolt of energy straight to his core. Everything shifts in an instant, the playful teasing giving way to something more primal.

"Yeah," she replies, crossing the room with a sway to her hips that drives him wild. "It goes down to the hot tub."

His body reacts instantly. "I didn't bring trunks."

"Clothing is optional in this hot tub."

That's all he needs to hear. In a few swift steps, he's on her, lifting her onto his hips. His hand finds the back of her neck, the other gripping her ass, pressing her against him. His lips hover just above hers, teasing, driving her—and himself—crazy. "I think *this* is the hottest part of the house, Charlotte."

He carries her into the elevator, pinning her back against the glass as the doors close. Her leg drops around his, giving her leverage as she grinds against him. He can feel the heat radiating from her, even through their clothes, and it takes everything in him not to lose control right then and there.

Fucking hell, this woman knows exactly what she's doing. He holds her gaze, their lips just a breath apart. "Charlotte," he growls softly, "you don't have control tonight. You'll give it all to me. You can have it back only when I say."

Her eyes flash with defiance, but he can see her wolf stirring behind them. "Submitting isn't in my nature, Liam. We may get hurt tonight. My wolf doesn't let go of control easily."

Good. That's exactly what he wants. Slowly, he moves his lips to her neck, inhaling deeply, letting her scent fill his lungs. "Your scent is intoxicating." His wolf stirs just beneath the surface, claws ready to tear through his skin. His tongue drags up from her collarbone, and when she tilts her head back, exposing her neck, he knows—she's giving in.

He rolls the tip of his finger over her nipple through her shirt, feeling her arch into him. *Perfection.* "Woman, I'd bleed for you," he murmurs, his voice thick with hunger.

Her chest rises and falls quickly, her breath mingling with his, but he holds back, keeping her on the edge. He closes his eyes, digging deep for control, but every part of him wants to devour her. He presses her harder against the glass, feeling her heat, her need, and it drives him wild. *I'm going to ruin you for anyone else,* knowing it's true.

The elevator doors slide open, revealing the stunning black marble hot tub, the lights shifting with the music. *You Put a Spell on Me* plays softly, and it's like the universe is in sync with them tonight.

Liam sets her down on her feet, his hands lingering on her body. "Perfect timing for that song," he whispers, his fingers already slipping beneath the hem of her shirt. But he waits, watching her, needing her permission.

Charlotte lifts her chin in silent agreement, and he pulls the shirt up and over her head, letting it drop to the floor. His thumb grazes her bottom lip, then follows the curve of her jaw until his hand finds the back of her neck. He yanks her close but stops just before their mouths meet. "I'm going to taste every inch of your body tonight, Charlotte," he promises, then crushes his lips to hers.

The kiss is hard, claiming. Tongues collide, and she tastes like dark chocolate and orange peels. His restraint is slipping fast. Hooking his thumbs into the waistband of her leggings, he pulls them down to her ankles, finding no underwear beneath. *Fuck, she's perfect.*

"Thank you, Charlotte," he mutters, his eyes raking over her naked form. He slowly undresses, watching her as she watches him. *Does she like what she sees?*

"You're gorgeous, Liam," she whispers, and it's like those words give him life.

Liam gently grabs her hand and leads her into the hot tub, the steam swirling around them. He sits, pulling Charlotte into his lap as her hips lift instinctively, seeking more. But he shakes his head, a wicked smile playing on his lips. "No, darlin'. I know what you want, but I'm going to make you come a few times first."

The tension between them is electric, humming under their skin. He bends down, pulling her perfect nipple into his mouth as his hand slides underwater, fingers parting her folds and finding the spot that makes her gasp. A moan escapes her lips when his fingers slide inside her, his thumb circling the swollen bud of nerves.

His body is on fire, but he's laser-focused on hers. "You're perfect," he breathes against her skin. "So hot. So wet. I'm going to make you come." His fingers thrust in and out, his thumb working slow, deliberate circles. "Then I'll carry you to bed and taste every inch of you."

She digs her nails into his back, her breath catching. When he pulls his fingers out, bringing them to his lips, he sucks her from them, groaning as his eyes flutter closed. "You take my breath away."

Charlotte's nails pierce deeper into his skin, but he doesn't mind. He slides his fingers back into her. "You make me see red, Charlotte. Everything burns when I'm near you." His voice trembles when her hand wraps around his dick, stroking him in time with his rhythm. The sensation nearly undoes him. His teeth sink into her nipple, and her whimper is the sweetest sound he's ever heard.

"My control is slipping," he warns, his voice thick. "You've woken something in me that's been dormant for too long."

"I never said I wanted gentle," she replies, her voice husky with desire. "I want you to take me. To a place where nothing else matters, where I don't have to think—just feel."

That's all he needs to hear. In one fluid motion, he stands, lifting her effortlessly, her legs wrapped around him. The plan to tease her, to draw it out, vanishes. He needs her now. He takes her to the outdoor table, flipping her around so her perfect ass is exposed to him. He swipes the dishes off, not caring where they land. "I'm going to fuck you so many times tonight, but if I don't get inside you now, I'm going to lose it."

She lifts her hips, wordlessly inviting him. He spits on his fingers, slicking her entrance before guiding himself in. Her hips wiggle in anticipation, driving him wild. He thrusts hard, burying himself to the hilt. Slowly, he pulls out, gripping her hips tightly, and then slams back in, a groan ripping from his chest.

"Charlotte, you're incredible. Being inside you..." His words trail off as the pleasure builds. "Fuck, I'm not done yet, and I already can't wait to do this again."

His pace quickens, each thrust deeper, harder. Charlotte clings to the table, trying to maintain control, but he can tell she's holding back. He wraps his hand in her silky black hair, pulling her head back just enough to whisper against her ear, "Give in, Red. I'll make you scream my name. Maybe not this time, but by the end of tonight, you'll scream it."

The wet slap of their bodies echoes through the air, amplifying the heat simmering between them. Liam's grip tightens on her hips as he watches Charlotte draped over the table, her back arched, her hair falling in waves over her shoulders. Each thrust pulls a small gasp from her, and he feels a fierce possessiveness rising in his chest, the primal need to claim her fully.

Her skin is flushed, each shiver under his touch feeding his own urgency. "I'm close," he growls, leaning over her, his voice thick with desire. "Going to put my scent in you," he murmurs, voice rough. *Let everyone know you're mine*, he thinks, but keeps that part tucked away for now. "Fuck Charlotte, tell me. Tell me I'm doing what you need." She cries out, her body trembling beneath him, clinging to the edge of the table as if it's her only anchor. He feels her surrender, her complete trust, and it sends him over the edge, raw and unrestrained.

That's all it takes. He thrusts deep, three more times, his release crashing through him. His hands move up and down her back as their breathing slows, both of them still trembling from the force of their release.

Rubbing her hip where his thumb left a mark, he checks her. "Are you okay, Red? Did I hurt you?"

Charlotte inches up onto her elbows, looking over her shoulder with a smirk. "Nerd. It takes a lot more than that to hurt me." Her eyes glint with satisfaction. "But that was fucking amazing."

"This is just a water break, Red." Liam steps back, admiring the way his seed glistens between her legs. Her look over her shoulder reignites the fire in him. His dick stands at attention, his wolf just beneath the surface. His voice drops to a growl. "Let's go. Break's over."

He scoops her up, tossing her playfully over his shoulder as they head back to the elevator.

Later, as the orgasm fog starts to clear, Liam feels Charlotte stir. He quickly reaches out, grabbing her arm and pulling her down next to him. "Where do you think you're going, Red Rock Queen?" His breath is hot against her ear.

"I was going to get a drink of water. You made me scream 'nerd' so many times I'm parched." She looks over her shoulder, raising an eyebrow that makes his heart race.

"Okay, but bring me some too." He rolls onto his back, hands behind his head, watching her saunter to the wet bar across the room.

"Water? Soda? Pedialyte?" she asks with a grin, opening the fridge.

"Water, please." He watches her move, her hips swaying

in a way that makes him want to pull her back into bed. "I appreciate the guest room, but after tonight? I think I've earned co-ownership of this bed."

Charlotte hands him a bottle of water, smirking. "Is that so? Is that an Oregon thing or a nerd thing?"

"Nah," he says, taking a swig of water. "I just don't want to mess up another room. Isabell might kick my ass if I create more work for her."

"That's fair." She sets her water on the nightstand, then slides back into bed, facing him. "Liam, I think my wolf would like it if you stayed the night."

"Just your wolf?" He brushes a few strands of hair from her face, his touch lingering.

"No, I want you to stay too. I haven't had a man stay the night... ever. I might snore."

"The snoring will help me find my way back to you if I roll away." He rolls flat on his back, spreading his arms out wide. "Seriously, is this the biggest bed ever made?"

"Stop that, you're pulling the sheets." Charlotte laughs, giving him a playful shove. "It has to be, right? Our designer picked it out. We told him to make everything look incredible and functional, so this is what I got."

They fall quiet, lying next to each other, the air between them thick with unspoken things. Liam's heart skips a beat. His wolf hasn't been this quiet in years. There's peace here, with her. So many questions swirl in his mind, but he doesn't want to scare her off—hell, he doesn't want to scare himself.

Charlotte breaks the silence, her eyes falling to his chest. "Can I ask you something personal?"

He gently lifts her chin, making her look at him. "Charlotte, you've got my scent all over you. You can ask me anything. And never drop your eyes for anyone. You're a queen, and people bow to you."

Her lips twitch at his words, but she holds his gaze. "Will you tell me about the accident that made you a lone wolf?"

Liam takes a deep breath, knowing this question was coming. He's braced for it, but the words still feel heavy. "I was mated. Her name was Sophie." His eyes lock onto Charlotte's, watching her realization hit like a wave.

"Oh," she says softly, her voice tinged with understanding but not pity. He senses she's unsure how to respond, so he pushes through.

"Sophie was killed in a car accident," he continues, the words flowing more easily than he expected. "It was a shock to the whole pack. We heal fast, but her injuries were too severe—she lost so much blood that her healing couldn't keep up." He pauses, drawing in a deep breath as he tries to gauge Charlotte's reaction. Then, with a bit more control, he continues, "I tried to stay with the pack, to keep going without her, but every place... every face reminded me of her. It was too much. Six months ago, I left. And three months after that, I felt the pack bond break." He glances down, his fingers tracing the curve of Charlotte's hip. "I miss them, but I don't miss the pity looks or the constant 'How are you holding up?' questions.

And I definitely don't miss the memories ambushing me every time I turned a corner."

"I'm so sorry, Liam." Her hand finds his cheek, and her touch is grounding, filled with respect and empathy, not pity. "I've had my share of broken bonds, but never a mate. I can't imagine how empty that must've felt. The fact that you're here, sharing this with me, it shows more strength than most people could ever muster."

Her gaze holds his, and for a moment, everything feels

clear. She sees him—not just the lone wolf, but the man beneath the scars.

"My turn?" He tries to lighten the moment, his smirk barely masking the vulnerability still lingering.

"I suppose it's only fair." Charlotte's lips twitch into a small smile, but there's hesitation in her eyes. "I'm not great at talking about things I don't want to, but I'll try."

Liam pulls the sheet over her head with a playful grin. "Hey!" She protests, her voice muffled under the covers.

He chuckles, knowing this question is going to push her, and she'll need the illusion of safety. "How did you become the Alpha of an all-female pack in the middle of the desert?"

Charlotte groans from beneath the sheets. "Leave it to you to ask the tough one right out of the gate." She peeks out, pulling the sheet down just enough to meet his eyes. "Alright, here's the cliff note version."

She sighs, sinking back against the pillows. "Harper, Jade, and I grew up in the Sidney Pack."

"Wait, not Luna?" Liam cuts in, surprised.

The amber gleam of her wolf shines through her eyes for a moment. "No. Luna joined us later. That's a story for another time—trust me, it'll make your wolf want to kill."

His shock registers, but he stays quiet, sensing the weight of her past.

"Our Alpha, my father, believed in the old ways—the Elder laws. The men were everything, and women were just... servants. I'm guessing it was similar to what you described with Maddy."

Liam nods, his brow furrowed. "Yeah, exactly like that. Maddy was 'promised' to a male she didn't even know."

"My father hated everyone and everything," Charlotte continues, her voice harder now. "He wasn't even a narcissist —I don't think he loved himself enough to be. His anger fueled him, and he took it out on my mother for simply existing. As I got older and my alpha powers started showing, that rage turned on me. We were caught in this vicious cycle. Every time he beat me, my wolf grew stronger, and that only made him angrier."

Liam watches as she sits up, reaching for her water. She takes a long drink, her throat tight with the memories. "Harper's dad helped us escape. He found a pack willing to take us in—the Black Canyon Pack in Wyoming. They taught us how to survive, how to fight. They made us into the women we are today."

Liam's heart clenches, his wolf growling softly at the thought of someone daring to hurt Charlotte. "I've heard of the Black Canyon's. Their Alpha's a legend—no one crosses her."

Charlotte smiles, the admiration clear on her face. "She's incredible. I would've died for her, no question. She offered us a place in her pack, but my wolf wasn't built to serve. She wanted to lead. After we left, my father found me again."

Liam feels her body tense beside him, and instinctively he rolls to his back, pulling her onto his chest, his arms wrapped tight around her. He breathes in her scent, trying to calm both of their wolves.

"I killed him." Her words are barely above a whisper, but the weight of them lands square on his chest. "I killed my father, Liam, and I felt nothing. Not relief, not anger, nothing. Harper says the feelings will come someday, but they haven't yet."

She takes a deep breath, her fingers tracing circles on his chest.

"After that, I had to decide what to do with the Sidney Pack. I didn't want to lead them, but they needed change, and I knew a female Alpha would be too much for them to handle. So, we found a male to help them adapt, and we left. We came to Vegas, not intending to start a sanctuary like Black Canyon, but then we met Luna. She needed us, and we needed her. Our pack grew to fifteen at one point... and then we lost some."

Her voice grows softer. "I miss them so much. It's like I have these empty shelves inside me, just waiting for the books to be returned."

"I know." Liam's voice is quiet, his thumb brushing along her jawline. "Bonds are a blessing and a curse."

He tucks a strand of hair behind her ear, his touch gentle. "Thank you for sharing that, Charlotte. I know that wasn't easy."

He pauses, gathering his thoughts. "That's why being a lone wolf felt so... right. No pack, no talking, no pain. But, honestly? That's just the lie I tell myself. The truth is, I hurt every day. I just tell myself that avoiding the bonds makes it easier, but it doesn't. The love I lost... even death couldn't take that away."

Liam tucks Charlotte's hair behind her ear, his hand lingering at her cheek. He doesn't say anything, just lets the moment stretch between them, heavy with the stories they've just shared. The space feels different now—quieter, more honest, like they've crossed into something deeper.

For the first time in a long while, Charlotte doesn't feel the weight of her Alpha title pressing down on her. Here, in the quiet of the night, with Liam's arms around her, she can just be. She doesn't have to be the strong one, doesn't have to lead. The vulnerability is terrifying, but it's also freeing. She feels her wolf stir under the surface, the same restlessness she's been fighting, but now there's something new—a sense of peace that she hasn't known in years.

Liam shifts beneath her, his arms tightening around her,

as if he feels the same. His wolf, calm but protective, mirrors hers. The silence between them isn't heavy, it's easy, comfortable.

"I've always been the one to protect everyone," Charlotte says softly, surprising herself with the confession. "It's hard to let someone in, even harder to admit I might need someone."

Liam's hand moves gently down her back, soothing and steady. "You're strong, Char, but no one is invincible. We all need someone to lean on."

Charlotte exhales, the truth of his words hitting harder than she expects. She's spent so long building walls, guarding her heart, that she's forgotten what it feels like to let someone in. And now, with Liam, those walls are crumbling faster than she can stop them. She doesn't know if that's a good thing or if she should be scared out of her mind.

She looks up at him, her wolf whispering something she's not ready to hear. *Mate.*

His dark eyes meet hers, searching, and for a moment, it feels like he's waiting for her to say something, to acknowledge the shift between them. But she can't. Not yet.

"I'm not good at this," she admits, her voice barely above a whisper. "I don't know how to just... let go."

Liam smiles softly, brushing his thumb across her cheek. "You don't have to be good at it. You just have to let yourself feel it."

The simplicity of his words strikes something deep inside her. She's spent so long burying her emotions, focusing on survival, that she's forgotten what it feels like to *feel*—to just be present in a moment with someone who sees her, not as an Alpha, but as a woman.

And Liam? He's not asking her to be anything other than

who she is. He's giving her space to breathe, to be vulnerable without judgment. It's the kind of safety she's craved, but never thought she'd find.

"I'm not sure I know how to do that." Her voice cracks slightly, the weight of everything she's held back pressing against her chest.

Liam leans down, pressing his forehead against hers. "Then let me help you. We can take it slow. You don't have to carry the weight of the world alone, Red."

Her heart stutters, her wolf quiet for the first time in what feels like forever. *Mate,* it whispers again, more insistent this time. She closes her eyes, willing herself to breathe, to accept this moment for what it is.

But her mind is still a battlefield, torn between wanting to feel, to let Liam in, and the fear that she'll lose herself in the process. She's been strong for so long—she doesn't know how to be anything else. But with Liam, maybe—just maybe—she can learn.

"I don't want to lose myself," she admits, her voice barely audible, the fear laced in every word.

"You won't." His voice is firm but gentle, his fingers tracing down her arm in soft strokes.

The promise settles between them, heavy with meaning. For the first time, Charlotte thinks she might actually believe him. She might actually let herself trust someone else with the parts of her she's always kept hidden.

As the night stretches on, they stay wrapped up in each other, neither speaking. The weight of their shared stories hangs in the air, but it doesn't suffocate—it heals. Charlotte feels her walls lowering, brick by brick, as Liam's warmth seeps into her skin.

As sleep starts to claim her, Charlotte knows one thing

for certain: whatever happens next, she's not in this alone. Not anymore.

But with that certainty comes another. The weight of Spencer's proposal still lingers in the back of her mind, the practical choice for her pack, for her future. But lying here, wrapped in Liam's warmth, she feels something deeper stirring inside her. Something instinctual, something true.

Her wolf hums quietly beneath the surface, steady and calm in a way it's never been. *Mate.* The word whispers again, soft but undeniable.

Spencer's offer had made sense at the time—an alliance of strength, security for her pack. It was logical, and Charlotte had always been a leader who put her pack first. But logic doesn't fill the empty spaces inside her, and it doesn't ignite the fire burning between her and Liam.

She thought Spencer's proposal would solve everything, but now? Now, she knows that path was never meant for her. She can't give Spencer something she doesn't feel. The connection she needs isn't born out of duty or strategy—it's this. This messy, intense, undeniable pull toward the man lying next to her.

Liam shifts slightly, his arm tightening around her, as if he senses her thoughts. Her heart races at the realization— *she's already made her choice.*

With a soft sigh, Charlotte decides she'll talk to Spencer soon, explain that while she values his offer, she can't accept it. She's found something else, something real. And though it scares her to admit it, even to herself, she's not turning back.

Whatever happens next, she's made her choice. And it's Liam.

I AM BAMBOO

L iam jolts upright in bed, heart racing as his phone rings. Maddy's name flashes on the screen, igniting instant panic.

"Madaline!"

"Liam, I need you." Her voice trembles, each word drenched in fear. "I took Avery, and we ran. I'm in the safe spot. Please, Liam, I'm ready. Please, come get me. I'll go anywhere—just get me away from him."

Liam is already out of bed, yanking on his jeans. "Breathe, Maddy. Stay calm. I need you to breathe for me, okay?" His voice stays steady, but inside, a storm rages.

"He was going to kill me this time, Liam." Her voice cracks, raw and broken. "It was bad."

His chest tightens, and he pulls a black shirt over his head, barely registering Charlotte stirring beside him. The fear in Maddy's voice claws at him, sharp and unrelenting. "I'm in Vegas right now, but I'm leaving. I'll be there in a few hours. Stay in the cave. Is it still a secret?"

"I think so," she whispers. "I don't think he followed me, but I'm scared. I'm really scared."

"You're safe right now," he reassures her, grabbing his boots, his fingers shaking as he laces them up. "Don't leave the cave until I get there. Do you hear me?"

"Please hurry," she sobs. "I don't know what he'll do if he finds us."

"You need to save your battery. I'm hanging up, but I'm on my way. I love you, Maddy. We'll get through this." He pauses, softening his voice. "Say it with me. You ready?"

A brief silence, then, together: "I am bamboo." A promise. Their bond, unbreakable.

The call ends. Liam shoves his phone into his pocket, his movements sharp, focused. "I'm sorry, but I have to go," he says tightly, his mind already racing toward the road ahead.

"Of course you do." Charlotte's voice is steady, though he can hear an undercurrent of something more. "I have friends up North. I'll call them, see if they can help. They might reach her faster."

Liam stops, hand hovering near the door. Her offer isn't casual—it's a risk. She's willing to step into his chaos for someone she doesn't even know. The weight of that hits harder than he expects.

Turning slightly, his gaze softens. "I appreciate it, but this guy... he's dangerous. I don't want your friends getting hurt." His voice is firm, protective, and not just for Maddy. "I'll call you once I'm on the road."

Without thinking, he leans down, capturing her lips in a kiss that's more than just a goodbye. It's quick but heavy, filled with everything he can't say. When he pulls back, he rests his forehead against hers. "Thank you for showing me the part of you no one else sees. I don't deserve your secrets, but I'll guard them with my life."

The truth in his words is startling, even to him. But there's no time to dwell on it now.

As he moves toward the door, her voice reaches him again. "Liam." It's soft, tugging at him. He stops, his hand tightening on the door handle.

"Bring your sister and her friend here," she says. "The Red Rocks will protect them."

The weight of her offer sinks into him—her pack, her home, her sanctuary—and it's almost too much. He tugs the brim of his cap lower, a flimsy shield against the storm inside.

His throat tightens, and his mind spins: fear of failing Maddy, guilt for considering Charlotte's offer, and emotions he doesn't have time to unpack. He feels her eyes on him, steady and unflinching. All he can manage is a quick nod—a silent thanks.

The door clicks shut behind him, unnervingly final. Outside, the cool air bites at his skin, but it doesn't lighten the weight pressing on his chest.

His promise to Maddy drives him forward, but leaving Charlotte claws at his resolve.

Still, he doesn't look back. He can't.

DEAL?

Charlotte isn't sure how long she's been lying there, staring at the ceiling. The weight of her decisions presses down, each scenario running through her mind like an endless film reel. She grabs her phone, her thumb hovering over the map app, but a random thought derails her focus.

I am bamboo.

Liam's words echo in her mind, pulling her into a new line of thought. She types "bamboo" into the search bar, curiosity taking over. Resilient. Strong but flexible. The fastest-growing plant in the world. He wasn't just trying to calm Maddy—he was empowering her. Giving her the strength to endure.

A quiet realization settles over her. This man isn't just rare—he's necessary. The world needs Liam, whether it knows it or not.

Switching back to the map app, she punches in a destination: Gold Beach. The travel time stares back at her. Spencer. He could get there faster.

It's 2 a.m., but she doesn't hesitate. She dials.

The phone rings once. Twice. By the third ring, she's ready to hang up when Spencer's groggy voice finally comes through.

"Hey, Charlotte. I was beginning to think you'd forgotten about me."

Her immediate thought—*I wish I could be that lucky*—stays locked in her head where it belongs. Instead, she says, "Hey, Spencer. I'm willing to make the deal—on one condition."

There's rustling on the other end, a sign he's waking up.

"Go on," he says, more alert now.

"I need your help. A friend's sister is in trouble, up in Oregon. My friend left Vegas just now, but you could get there faster."

He pauses. "What kind of trouble?"

"Her mate's a piece of shit with old-fashioned views on females," Charlotte growls, her wolf stirring beneath the surface. "She ran tonight. She's hiding in a cave with another female—could be a child, could be a friend, I don't know. But she's terrified. She's sure he'll kill her if he finds her."

Silence stretches for a moment, heavy. Then Spencer clicks his tongue.

"So, we may end up with blood on our hands?" His voice sharpens, all traces of sleep gone.

"Yes," Charlotte says flatly.

A low chuckle rumbles through the phone. "Hell yeah. My males could use a good fight. Taking down abusive shifters is a favorite pastime around here. Where am I headed?"

Relief loosens the knot in her chest. She exhales slowly. "I'll get the exact location from Liam, and we'll work out the details. There are... other things we need to discuss too."

Spencer's tone softens, though his words remain firm. "Charlotte, listen. We'll do this—not because of the deal, but because it's the right thing to do. We don't tolerate abuse. Let's get these women safe. After that, we'll talk. Cool?"

Her shoulders drop. "Cool." She pauses, sincerity breaking through. "Spencer... thank you."

Setting her phone down, Charlotte feels the weight lift, if only slightly. Maddy will be safe soon, and her future—uncertain as it is—will be with an honorable man.

Even if there's no love between them, there will be respect.

For now, that's enough.

It's been a few hours since she sent Spencer the details. Charlotte sits on the plush couch in her room, the silence offering little comfort as her mind churns through possible futures. Aligning the Red Rocks with the Humboldt Pack would be a bold step—one not unlike the risks she'd taken before. Trusting another pack wasn't new to her, but it was never easy. Her thoughts drift back to the pack that gave her and her sisters sanctuary, the one that molded her into the Alpha she is now.

Black Canyon. The name alone invokes a sense of safety and power, an oasis amidst the chaos of her youth. She closes her eyes and lets the memories take over, pulling her back to the harsh terrain of Wyoming. The Black Canyon Alpha was unlike anyone she'd ever met. Strong, fierce, and utterly uncompromising, she ruled not through fear but through respect.

Charlotte can still feel the sting of her muscles, the burn in her lungs from those early days of training.

"Shifting is more than survival—it's a weapon," the Alpha would say. *"Use your size to your advantage. You're smaller than the males, but that means you're faster. Never let a larger opponent pin you down."*

They'd train for hours in the snow-covered hills, learning how to shift in the blink of an eye. Charlotte remembers the first time she shifted mid-leap, knocking Harper to the ground, using her momentum to flip her opponent.

"You're going to be Alpha one day, Charlotte," Lyla would say, her voice fierce and unwavering, that wild glint in her eyes. *"But it's not about strength—it's about strategy. Know when to strike and when to retreat. Let them think they've won until you tear their throats out—or better yet, outsmart them."*

"A true Alpha doesn't lead because she's the strongest or knows everything. Always listen to those around you. Let your pack's knowledge and experience sharpen your instincts. Knowledge is power, and power isn't just safety—it's freedom."

Charlotte shifts in her seat, the weight of her memory

settling heavily on her chest. Her fingers trace the edge of her coffee mug, the warmth grounding her against the cold reality of the past. She exhales slowly, her gaze drifting to the window.

"But freedom isn't the ability to say or do whatever you want. True freedom is the strength to say what needs to be said, to do what needs to be done, and to accept the consequences with your head held high."

"That's what I'm doing for you right now, Charlotte," Lyla's voice echoes in her mind, steady and unyielding. *"I'm showing you that it's possible to rise, no matter how far you've fallen. And one day, you'll do the same for someone else. It's not about being the strongest or the smartest—it's about standing back up, over and over again, even when it feels impossible."*

"The greatest thing we can do in this life is to reach out a hand when someone else needs it, to remind them they're not alone. We're stronger together—always. That's what it means to be a pack. That's how we heal. That's how we endure. And that's what it means to truly live."

The words sent a chill through Charlotte, her stomach twisting into knots. Alpha? Her? The idea had scared the pants off her back then, and at times, it still does. She hadn't been able to picture herself leading a conversation, let alone a pack. Confidence had been as foreign to her as peace, and the thought of holding that kind of power had felt more like a curse than an honor. She had stared at Lyla in disbelief, her chest tight, certain the older woman was either joking or horribly mistaken.

But Lyla's gaze had remained steady, unwavering, as if she could already see the Alpha Charlotte didn't yet believe she could become.

The lessons had been relentless but necessary. Every bruise, every drop of blood shed, had sharpened her instincts. The scars etched into her skin became badges of honor. Black Canyon didn't just teach them to survive—they taught them to conquer.

But the memories weren't all triumph. Her mind drifts to the second most important decision of her life. Charlotte was faced with a choice to stay or to go. Lyla had offered her a place, a home, a chance to belong. Her voice had been calm yet commanding, the kind that demanded attention without raising in volume.

"You have a choice, Charlotte."

Lyla had said, her gaze unwavering.

"Stay, grow with us, become part of this family. Or leave and carve out a place of your own. Both paths have their trials, but you have the strength to face either."

Charlotte had wanted to stay. Desperately. But even then, her wolf had wrestled with the idea, pacing, growling, the urge to challenge Lyla simmering beneath the surface. Lyla had been everything Charlotte aspired to be—wise, fair, unshakably strong. She could never betray that. Never challenge the Alpha who had given her hope when she'd had none.

"You already know your path,"

Lyla had said softly, seeing the conflict etched in Charlotte's features.

"Trust your instincts. They won't lead you astray."

Those words had stayed with her, a beacon in the darkest moments. Black Canyon had been the foundation that rebuilt her, transforming a broken girl cowering under a cruel father's rule into the Alpha she is today.

Now, as Charlotte sits in the silence of her room, she realizes this moment marks the third time in her life she's faced this choice. Stay or go. It feels heavier this time, the stakes impossibly high—not just for her, but for her pack, her future, and the fragile ties she's building with Liam.

The question looms larger than ever, pressing on her chest. What kind of Alpha—what kind of woman—does she want to be?

The memory steels her resolve. Every lesson, every sacrifice, every decision—leading to this moment. Her phone vibrates against the table, pulling her out of the past. She taps the speakerphone and leans back.

"Hey, nerd. You doing okay?"

"I'm fine, but getting tired. Want to talk and keep me awake? Just... don't talk dirty, Red. I need to hydrate properly before we do that again." She can hear the teasing in his voice. "Maybe I should've gone with the Pedialyte."

Charlotte smirks, dragging out her words. "Soooooooo... make it as dirty as possible?" She hits send on a text.

He laughs. "Did you just text me? Please let it be a booby pic. Please, oh please."

"Check it later when you're not driving. Where are you?"

"I think I'm north of Tonopah. Still got a few hours to go. And hey, thanks for calling your friend—even though I said not to. You really are terrible at following orders."

"I give them, Liam, not follow them. Well... unless we're in bed." The words slip out before she can stop them, and she's not quite sure what to make of it.

"Yeah, you listened pretty well." There's that wicked smile in his voice, but then his tone shifts. "Heard from your friends yet?"

"Not yet. Spencer said they were about three and a half hours out, so it could be anytime now. They're good guys. They'll protect the girls." She hears a low growl come through the phone.

"Charlotte." His voice is cautious. "Can I ask how you

know these guys? I know you hear my wolf... so, let's just say I'm asking for a friend."

Rolling her eyes, she was waiting for this. "You remember the night we ran into each other on the strip?"

"Of course. I got to make out with you in your truck like a teenager. That night's seared into my brain."

His honesty sends warmth through her, but she focuses. "I was there meeting with Lucas Williams from the Humboldt Pack. He wanted to set up a meeting with his Alpha to extend an offer."

"I take it you took the meeting? What was the offer?" His voice is still laced with suspicion.

"He offered unity. The Humboldts want to help with our Cascade problem." Charlotte carefully sidesteps the whole truth—she's not ready to give that piece away just yet.

Liam's growl deepens. "Was the guy at the gym Lucas? The one who didn't really engage with you?"

"Oh, you caught that, huh?" Charlotte clears her throat, then continues. "Yeah, Lucas has been spying on the Cascades, gathering intel. As soon as he figured out what they were planning here in Vegas, he got his Alpha involved." Silence stretches between them, and Charlotte knows she's skating on thin ice. Liam's wolf is still on edge, and he's piecing things together.

"So... this Alpha?" Liam prods.

"Spencer," Charlotte supplies quickly.

"Fine. Spencer. He just offered to help you out of the kindness of his heart?"

Shit. "Yeah, something like that." Seeing her chance to divert, Charlotte blurts, "Can I tell you a secret?"

"Oh, I love secrets, Red. You know I'll protect all of yours."

"Well, this one isn't really mine... and it's not exactly a

secret, more of an unconfirmed fact." Charlotte takes a sip of coffee, savoring the suspense. "You're not the only guy who's caught the eye of a Red Rock."

Liam's voice perks up. "Don't leave me hanging. It's Luna, right? It has to be Luna. Guys would line up for her."

"Nope. Harper."

"What? Really?" He whistles. "Wait, don't tell me... the spy?"

"Damn, nerd, you're quick. Yep, Lucas Williams. Apparently, they met just before the attack at the gym. Harper thinks she's found her mate."

"No shit. Her mate? That's big. You cool with that? She might want to leave."

Charlotte lets out a heavy breath. "I know. But Harper's happiness means everything to me. She's been saving me since we were pups. If she's got a shot at real happiness, who am I—or this pack—to stand in the way?"

Liam clicks his tongue. "Well, if she's found her mate, staying away won't be an option for long."

Charlotte giggles. "Oh, I know. I think he's here right now."

"What? I thought I smelled something out of place when I got to the bottom of the stairs, but Isabell distracted me with a bag full of food. By the way, after we talk about Harper, can we discuss how Isabell does that?"

Charlotte laughs, running a hand through her hair as she takes a deep breath. "Harper deserves the world. And yes, we'll dive into the enigma of Isabell once I crack the code myself." Shifting on the couch, leaning back as she speaks. "Harper's family was different from the rest of the pack. Her dad didn't believe in the old ways. He was Jade's and my safe place. We'd go there to get patched up and heal before going home again." Her wolf stirs beneath the surface, restless, as the memories flood back. "He had to put on an act, pretend to be tough in front of others, but it tore him up inside. I can still picture him, crying as he held her mom, apologizing like he could make up for it."

"My old pack went through something similar when Brian became Alpha," he says. "Change is tough on the older wolves. Hard to teach them new tricks." His dry chuckle filters through, but there's an undercurrent she doesn't miss—memories he's not sharing.

Charlotte takes a sip from the mug she is holding, listening as he continues. "There were plenty of males who didn't want to be part of the old patriarchy anymore. They wanted real partnerships with their mates. But old habits? They don't die easy. Even with Brian not just giving them permission to change, but *demanding* it."

She leans her head against the couch, her eyes fixed on the darkened room in front of her. She's seen what he's talking about—wolves clinging to traditions that crush everything around them.

Liam exhales sharply, and she hears the faint hum of his Bronco in the background. "He made it clear that every female deserved respect, not just because they were part of the pack, but because they were strong, capable wolves in their own right. Most of us got it. Some of the older ones, though…" His voice tightens, and she knows that frustration all too well. "They couldn't—or wouldn't—break the cycle."

Charlotte shifts, setting her coffee mug on the side table. She wonders what it must've been like for Liam, watching Brian fight against centuries of conditioning. Hell, her own pack had its struggles with that same damn cycle.

"It wasn't just about rules," Liam says, his tone softening like the thought pulls at him. "It was about unlearning everything they'd been taught to believe. The kind of thing that doesn't happen overnight. There were fights—hell, I lost count of how many times Brian had to step in and remind everyone what it meant to be a pack. Not just males and females, but partners. Equals."

His laugh is low and bitter. "Funny thing is, the ones who resisted the most were the first to crumble when their mates started walking away. Turns out, losing respect and love stings worse than claws."

Charlotte's fingers brush the edge of her phone, her thoughts pulling her deeper into his words. She doesn't respond, sensing he isn't quite done yet.

"It wasn't easy, but Brian stood his ground. And little by little, things changed. The males who wanted something better—they started leading by example. The rest? Well, the pack didn't have room for anyone who couldn't adapt."

Charlotte smiles faintly, the corners of her lips tugging upward as she shakes her head. Liam's voice, rough and tinged with weariness, fills the quiet room, but when she hears another yawn over the line, her smile fades.

"You still good?" she asks, her tone softening despite the teasing edge. "Did you grab some coffee or an energy drink? You're not going to be any help to Maddy if you crash before you get there."

Liam smirks, the sound unmistakable in his voice. "I'm okay. How about you? Thanks for staying up with me, even though you've got to be exhausted from the workout I gave you earlier."

Her phone chimes. Glancing at the screen, her smile widens, and a spark of relief lights in her chest. "Hang on... Yes! Spencer's got the girls."

"What?" Liam's voice cracks. "Your friend has Maddy?"

Charlotte nods, even though he can't see her. "Yep. He said he'll call you in a few minutes so you can talk to her.

Her phone died, but she's safe. Call me after, okay?" There's only silence. "Liam?"

Finally, he exhales. "I'm okay. I... I can't thank you enough, Charlotte. My heart's pounding out of my chest. I'll call you after I talk to her, then find a place to crash for a bit."

Hearing the relief in his voice makes her relax. "Okay, nerd. Talk soon."

MADDY IS SAFE

Maddy's small, trembling voice filters through his phone. "I'm ok, Liam."

Liam exhales, trying to steady the racing in his chest. "You gave me a scare this time, Maddy. I'm glad you're safe. Where are you?"

"Spencer brought us to a motel," she replies, her voice shaky, the weight of exhaustion and fear still clinging to her words.

Liam clenches his jaw, his mind still in overdrive. "But are you safe? Have these males treated you right?" His heart won't stop pounding until he sees her, holds her, but her answer will determine if he needs to act now.

"They were prepared," she says, sounding a little steadier. "They had water, blankets, protein bars... it's like they've done this before. Spencer, he's the Alpha, he's been sitting outside Avery's room, and there's another guy, Jaxson, outside mine. We're safe... for now." Her words are slow, but there's a touch of awe in them, like she's not used to being taken care of like this.

"Good," Liam murmurs, though the tension stays coiled

inside him. He softens his voice. "Maddy, who's Avery? I wanted to ask earlier, but it didn't seem important at the time. If you thought she needed to come with you, then that's enough for me, but who is she?"

A pause. "You don't remember meeting her? She's Leo's sister," Maddy says, voice growing a little stronger. "She moved in with us a year ago when her mate was killed in a territory battle. I couldn't leave her behind, Liam... he would've killed her, too."

The burn of anger surges through him, but he reins it in. "I'm glad you brought her. You did the right thing, Maddy. Listen, I've got a friend—Charlotte—she's the Alpha of an all-female pack. She's offering you both sanctuary, protection. You'll be safe there."

"An all-female pack?" Maddy's voice wavers with surprise. "Wow... I'll tell Avery tomorrow."

Liam's heart clenches at how fragile she sounds, this petite, battered female who has survived so much more than most could ever handle. He hates that she's still enduring. "Good. Get some rest. I'm going to crash for a bit myself," he lies, knowing full well there won't be any sleep for him. "I'll be there as soon as I can."

"Thank you, Liam. I love you. I can't wait for you to get here," Maddy says softly.

"Love you too, kid," Liam responds, his voice catching as he hears the door open and Maddy calling for Spencer.

A shuffling sound comes through the phone before Spencer speaks. "She's okay, man. I've got Jaxson outside her door. Even if that bastard caught our scent, he won't get close to these girls." Spencer's confidence is a balm, a temporary relief to Liam's gnawing worry.

Liam's voice turns low, almost feral. "I'm not stopping

until this is over. He's not going to get the chance to hurt them again. I'm going to make sure of it."

There's a pause on the other end, Spencer clearly understanding the beast that Liam's become. "You have my number if you need backup. But this is your kill, not mine."

"Thanks for going to get them. I owe you." His voice is tight, controlled rage simmering just below the surface. "I'll get there as soon as I'm done."

"You don't owe me anything. Just... kill him good," Spencer growls before the line clicks dead.

Liam stands there for a moment, staring at his phone, every nerve in his body alight with the need for action. The Humboldt Pack has proven their worth. He has to trust them with Maddy—for now. But there's only one thing on his mind, and that's putting Leo in the ground.

He dials Charlotte.

"Hey... is everything okay? Is she safe?" Her voice is thick with sleep, but concern seeps through.

"Spencer's got her. They're both safe at a motel," he replies, adrenaline still pumping, making his words come out fast. "I've got to go take care of the problem. It'll be a couple of days before I get there."

"Going after him?" Her voice sharpens, all traces of sleep gone.

"Yes."

"I don't blame you," she says, a quiet edge to her words. "I've killed men for hurting my sisters, too."

Her words settle something deep inside him, something raw and broken. "If something happens to me... will Maddy and Avery still be safe? Will you still offer them sanctuary?"

"Liam," her voice is firm, unwavering, "I'm not offering sanctuary because of you. I'm offering it because they're females who need protection. They need a place where they can heal. We all carry broken pieces in this house, but we hold each other up when the weight gets too heavy. That's what this pack is built on."

His breath catches. "You're... you're incredible, Charlotte. I'll do my best not to die."

She chuckles softly, and the sound wraps around him like a lifeline. "You're not going to die, nerd. I've seen you fight. You don't just win—you dominate. You'll be fine."

Her confidence in him builds a new layer of strength around his resolve. He smirks, leaning back against the car. "Thanks for the pep talk. Now, I'm off to jam out to the new Taylor Swift album. Have you heard it?"

"No, not yet," she replies with a small laugh.

Liam grins. "Well, you're missing out. Talk to you soon, Red."

PLANS WITHIN PLANS

I t's been two days since she last heard from Liam. The silence weighs heavy, a knot tightening in her chest.

Spencer texted late last night, saying the girls were safe and recovering, but there was no mention of Liam. She thought about asking but held back, not wanting to seem overly concerned—it felt too personal, too soon. Instead, she's left with her own nagging worry, pacing the edges of her mind. Bigger wolves to fry, she reminds herself, pushing thoughts of Liam aside—for now.

Tonight, she's the first to sit down for family dinner. Isabell had threatened to quit if they didn't start sitting down together as a family for meals, and no one dared call her bluff. The ladies shifted their schedules to make sure they were home by six, all because of Isabell's ultimatum. She wasn't one to make idle threats.

"What's for dinner, Isabell?" Charlotte asks, trying to distract herself as Isabell enters the dining room with plates and bowls lined up her arms like a balancing act.

"Spaghetti with meatballs, señorita." Isabell's voice is

calm as she fills the Lazy-Susan just as the rest of the pack—Harper, Luna, and Jade—trickle in, settling at the table.

"Holy shit, Isabell. I'm a chef de cuisine, and my food doesn't smell this good," Harper says, stopping dead in her tracks when she spots the spaghetti. "See, Luna! This is spaghetti, not that canned crap you try to pass off."

Luna shrugs nonchalantly, dropping into her chair while the others exchange glances.

There's a secret hanging in the air that none of them seem to know, except for Isabell. She approaches Luna, pressing kisses to each of her cheeks before leaning in to whisper something in her ear. Then, as swiftly as she entered, she disappears back into the kitchen.

Jade is the first to break the silence, eyeing Luna. "You good?"

Luna keeps her head down, voice low. "I had to let my beasts out today. I thought Isabell was at the store. Just wanted to give them a minute to breathe. But... she screamed 'El Diablo' and ran. I didn't mean to scare her... I hate scaring people."

The sadness in Luna's voice hits Charlotte hard, propelling her out of her chair. She moves to Luna's side, the others following suit, surrounding her. They lay their hands on her in a quiet, shared ritual they'd created long ago.

"Your beasts are good, Luna," Charlotte says, her voice firm. "You protect each other at all costs."

"The three of you were forged from fire," Harper adds, "Embrace the strength."

Jade squeezes Luna's shoulder, grinning. "You're a badass. Now lift your damn head up."

This ritual goes back to their days at Black Canyon. Even though they had been accepted by the pack, the bond between Charlotte, Jade, and Harper ran deeper. They could feel when each other's darkness threatened to overshadow the light. Wolves are tactile creatures, and through touch, they passed positive energy—reminding each other of their strength.

Luna finally lifts her head, eyes shining with gratitude. "Thanks, ladies. I know my beasts are strong. We've protected each other through fire. We just don't like scaring people we care about. But... Isabell is okay. I just needed that reminder—we're beautiful. I love you, pack." She stands, pulling them all into a tight group hug.

Jade pulls back first, a smirk on her face. "Alright, enough of this mushy shit. My food's getting cold."

Harper piles her plate with meatballs, laughing. "You know, I think Miles has been sniffing around again. I swear I saw him and that idiot Ethan at the casino earlier."

Charlotte's face hardens. "I saw them too. We need to be prepared for whatever they're planning. Jade, do you have any big clients this week?"

"Not this week. We've got a mid-level client coming in next, but Alison can handle it if needed." Jade shovels noodles into her mouth without missing a beat.

Charlotte turns to Harper and Luna. "How about you two? Anything that'll get screwed up if we have to go to war again?"

They both shake their heads, Harper smiling wide. "Menus are set for the month. I can kill a wolf any day you need." She chuckles before glancing at Isabell's masterpiece on the table. "Now, why the hell does her food taste better than mine?"

"Because you didn't cook it," Luna jokes, throwing her hands up. "No, I mean... food always tastes better when someone else makes it."

Harper stares at her for a moment, then bursts into laughter, the sound infectious as it spreads to Luna.

Dinner resumes with the usual banter, back-and-forth teasing and the shared ease of pack life. Charlotte fills the others in on Liam and the Humboldts, telling them about the two fragile females who will soon be joining them. She keeps the deal with Spencer to herself—for now.

Later, needing to burn off nervous energy, Charlotte heads to their small home gym. It's not as well-equipped as her main gym, but it's enough for the pack. She starts on the leg press, upping the weight, when Jade walks in.

"You good, Alpha?" Jade asks, dropping onto the bench press across from her.

"Not really," Charlotte admits, adjusting the weights with a sharp click. "I can't shake the feeling the Cascades are planning another attack. It's like they're circling, waiting. I wish we could just take the fight to them for once instead of waiting around."

Jade watches her for a moment, eyes narrowing in thought. "Maybe we can," she says, standing to rack the kettlebell with a heavy thud. "What if we flip the script? Set a trap. We create a fake event, something they can't resist. Luna can flood their emails with ads—make them think they're about to ambush us, but we control everything. They'll come to us—on our terms."

Charlotte pauses, hands stilling on the weights as she lets the idea sink in. The tension in her shoulders eases for the first time in days. "That's... not a bad idea," she muses, a slow grin spreading across her face. "We could rent a warehouse, make it look like I'm opening a new satellite gym. They'd think they're attacking us in public, but we'd have them right where we want them."

Jade mirrors her grin, the spark of a challenge lighting in

her eyes. "Exactly. We don't wait for them to make the first move. Let's hit them where it hurts."

"Let's get the others and talk this through," Charlotte says, her voice steady with newfound determination. "We need a solid plan."

Charlotte leans her head back, letting the jets of the hot tub work into the knots of tension that have been building for days. The ridiculous "space sound" of her phone's ringtone break the quiet.

"Hey nerd. Glad you're alive." She winces at the shake in her own voice.

"Hey, Red. Were you worried about me?"

Relief floods her body at the sound of his voice, sending shivers down her spine, even though she's submerged in the hundred-degree water. "Worried? Nah. Perturbed that I might never get that dick again? Yes."

"Oh, don't worry. You'll get it again. How about tomorrow?" His words melt the tension she's been carrying, easing into her like the heat from the water. "Can I still bring the girls down to you? They're pretty shaken up."

"Of course. I'll have Isabell get a couple of rooms ready," Charlotte says, climbing out of the hot tub, the cool night air kissing her damp skin. The soft splash of water as she steps out echoes through the phone, and she knows Liam hears it too.

"Charlotte, please tell me you're naked. Wait, even if you aren't, lie to me. You're naked in the hot tub, right?"

The playful tone in his voice sends warmth through her, a reminder of just how dangerous this man is to her resolve. The confidence he brings out in her is terrifying, igniting something deep inside she's not ready to face. He doesn't realize it yet, but he holds a power over her—a power she knows she'll have to push away if she's ever going to find peace with Spencer.

"I don't think I'll ever lie to you, Liam," she says, the truth slipping from her lips as naturally as the water dripping from her body. "I am naked, but tomorrow..." The sadness seeps into her voice, unbidden. "Tomorrow, we can't be together."

"Why? I get it, I'm a lone wolf and eventually, I'll have to leave your territory, but what's the harm in having a bit of fun?"

"You asked before about the offer. You knew there was more to it, didn't you?" She hesitates, the weight of her next words pressing down on her.

"Yes. What's the 'more'?" His voice darkens, a growl just beneath the surface.

"The deal was to mate and bond our packs together," she admits quietly, her voice tight as the words tear through her. Her wolf stirs violently beneath her skin, clawing at her insides, urging her to fight against this truth she's forced to speak. "I wasn't sure I was going to do it, but I made a deal of my own."

"What deal, Charlotte?" His voice sharpens, low and dangerous.

She can feel her wolf fighting, desperate to take control, to deny the arrangement she's made. "I knew Spencer could get to the girls faster. "So I told him if he kept them safe..." She exhales, the tension in her chest easing just enough to let her finish. "I'd take his deal."

The silence that follows is suffocating, the tension thick in the air. Her wolf tears at her chest, howling at the thought of giving up Liam, of mating with someone else. The beast inside her is in turmoil, and it takes everything in her to stay calm.

"I'll take care of this right now." His words are barely human, a deep snarl vibrating through the phone. She can almost see him shifting, his wolf clawing to the surface, ready to fight.

"What do you mean, you'll take care of it?" Panic laces her voice as her heart pounds, her wolf surging forward, frantic.

"I'm going to challenge him."

"Liam, wait..."

LET'S BE FRIENDS INSTEAD

"**S**pencer!" Liam's roar shakes the run-down motel, his vision clouded by pure rage. He stomps down the sidewalk, his mind only focused on finding Spencer. He wants the man to see the whites of his eyes when he challenges him—for his pack, and for Charlotte.

Spencer emerges from room 117, his brow furrowed. "What the fuck, dude?"

Liam's steps thunder down the hallway, each one fueled by the fury coursing through his veins. His voice, a low growl, drips with accusation. "Here I was, thinking you were just a nice guy helping out your friend," he snarls, not slowing down. "But really... you're exploiting her pack's vulnerability. Tying her to you just to gain more territory?" He stops abruptly, eyes narrowing as they land on the room number. "Isn't this Avery's room?" Liam's instincts sharpen, sensing Kai and Jaxson closing in. The protectiveness rolls off them, their wolves primed to defend their Alpha.

Before they can reach him, Spencer shoves Liam inside the room, raising his hand with a single commanding motion to his guards. "I got this," Spencer's Alpha power ripples through the air like a wall, halting the others in their tracks.

Spencer slams the door shut behind them, cutting off the hallway noise. He pushes past Liam, moving to the center of the room, placing himself squarely between Liam and Avery, who sits curled in the corner, her knees pulled tight to her chest. "You've got it all wrong, man. I mean, you got some of it right, but... things have changed."

Liam, still breathing hard from his earlier rage, narrows his gaze. "What the hell does that mean?"

Spencer glances over at Avery, his expression softening. "I think Avery is my mate. I'm forty-three years old, man. I thought fate forgot me, so yeah, I made that deal with Charlotte. I figured two older alphas could help each other out, but it wasn't anything more than that."

Liam pauses, taking in Spencer's protective stance in front of Avery, noticing the subtle shift in the room. Spencer wasn't trying to challenge him for Charlotte—he was guarding someone he now considered his own. The anger simmering inside Liam begins to cool as understanding sets in.

He looks around Spencer's broad chest to Avery. "Avery, I'm sorry. I didn't mean to scare you."

Her voice is small, shaky. "It's okay."

Spencer steps back, dropping his guard just a little. "I was going to call Charlotte tonight and let her know about Avery. I still want to align the packs. Those she-wolves are badass, and I think it's better to be on their good side." His shoulders relax, and he gives a small grin. "Especially with you on their side. You're fucking scary, man."

Liam drops his head, the tension easing from his muscles. "I was going to challenge you."

Spencer laughs, the sound breaking through the leftover

tension. "Fuuuuck. I'd rather be friends, man." He extends his hand.

Liam grabs Spencer's wrist, pulling him into a back-slapping hug. "And Spencer, you are a nice guy." Their laughter shifts the energy to something more relaxed.

Spencer pulls out of the manhug and smirks. "Alright, who's calling Charlotte to tell her what went down?"

Liam narrows his eyes. "I'm not doing it. You're the one who put her through all this."

Spencer crosses his arms, leaning back against the motel dresser. "You're the one that was going to challenge me, man. This one's on you."

A moment of silence passes before both men realize there's only one way to settle this.

"Roshambo?" Spencer suggests.

Liam chuckles, nodding. "Yeah, let's go."

They square off, standing too seriously for what's about to happen. Avery, though still wary, watches the two men with faint curiosity. It's the first time she's seen men have a civil confrontation—no threats, but as people trying to diffuse tension.

"One... two... three... shoot!" Spencer throws paper while Liam, grinning like a devil, throws scissors.

"Ha! Scissors beats paper!" Liam grins triumphantly.

Spencer shakes his head, laughing. "Best two out of three?"

Liam shrugs. "Alright. One more."

They reset, both shaking their fists in rhythm.

"One... two... three... shoot!" This time, Liam throws rock, and Spencer's scissors meet their doom.

Liam grins even wider, trying not to gloat too much. "Guess you're up, man."

Spencer groans dramatically. "You're killing me, but

fair's fair. I have a feeling she is going to be relieved she doesn't have to live with my sorry ass."

As Spencer dials Charlotte, Liam leaves the room knowing the inevitable fallout is coming. He knows Spencer's call is softening the blow, but he also knows Charlotte won't hold back when it's his turn.

A few moments later, "My Queen" flashes on Liam's phone.

He answers, leaning against the wall in the dimly lit motel corridor. "Hey, Red. On a scale of one to ten, how pissed are you?"

Charlotte's voice cuts through the line, sharp but laced with a dark edge of humor. "I was pissed earlier. Did you fucking see how many times I fucking called you?"

Liam feels the weight of her words settle over him, and for a moment, he pulls back, instinctively reacting to the authority in her tone. It's rare—her Alpha command hits him, making him shrug into himself, something he hasn't felt since the bond with his old pack broke. "You're lucky you won RoShamBo."

Liam smirks, pushing off the wall. "Well, it was best out of three." He knows his temper got the better of him, and that Charlotte doesn't need anyone swooping in to rescue her. "I was going to challenge him?"

There's a pause, her voice still carrying that edge. "That's what you said right before hanging up on me."

Liam sighs, rubbing the back of his neck. "I was ready. My temper just... took over. I wasn't thinking clearly."

"What would that have gotten you, Liam? Besides a pack you don't want?" she snaps, her voice tight with frustration. "It was stupid."

"You're right, it was stupid," he admits, "because I don't want that pack. But my wolf..." He takes a deep breath, feeling the words catch in his throat. "My wolf couldn't handle the idea of you mating with someone else, Red. If the deal was to align the packs through an Alpha pairing, it would have to be me, not him."

There's a long silence on the other end. When she finally speaks, her tone is unreadable. "You were going to take a pack just to make sure I didn't mate with Spencer?"

Liam straightens, feeling his chest swell with certainty. "Yeah. I was. And I hope you feel it too, Red. Because my dick is obsessed with you." He can't help the grin that spreads across his face, feeling the tension break.

Charlotte spits out a laugh on the other end, the sound instantly warming him. "Good. Because now that I'm not, sort of, engaged, I'd like a turn with that obsession. Someone wouldn't let me have a go last time."

Liam chuckles, the weight lifting off his shoulders. "Tomorrow, Red. I'm bringing it all. We'll be leaving early, but it'll still be late when we get there."

"Ok. I've asked the Humboldts to come back to Vegas too. We've got a plan to draw the Cascades to us, instead of waiting around. I'll explain to all of you when you get here."

"Guess I better get my ass to bed, then," Liam says with a yawn, stretching his arms above his head. "Long drive ahead."

"See you tomorrow night, Nerd," Charlotte says softly, before hanging up the phone.

MAYBE ENEMY'S OF MY
ENEMY CAN BE FRENEMIES?

The plan is coming together swiftly, each piece falling into place throughout the morning.

Jade secured a small abandoned warehouse on the outskirts of town, perfect for their fake event.

Luna crafts the marketing materials—emails, social media blasts, and flyers designed to lure the Cascades into their trap.

Charlotte arranges for a few pieces of old gym equipment to be delivered tomorrow, enough to make the setup look convincing. She knows in her gut that one of the Cascades is already watching, probably tracking every move they make.

Four hours ago, she got a text from Liam: "Are you hydrating?" The memory of it pulls a faint smile to her lips, but the tension quickly floods back. She paces the great room, her boots scuffing a divot into the marble floor. Isabell's going to lose it when she sees that.

"Hey, Char," Harper's voice cuts through the room as she enters, holding a mug of coffee in one hand and a bowl of cookie dough ice cream in the other. Her eyes sparkle with mischief, but there's concern in them too.

Charlotte stops mid-pace, eyeing the treats. "Damn girl, I swear you know me better than I know myself sometimes." She gratefully accepts the mug and bowl, sinking onto the cobalt blue chaise lounge with a sigh.

"I figured you could use some company. I could feel your anxiety from upstairs," Harper says softly, settling into the oversized white throne chair across from her.

Charlotte takes a bite of the ice cream, the sweetness soothing but not enough to calm her completely. "I didn't want to keep anyone else up. I'm just... I'm excited to see him, Harp. And that scares the shit out of me."

Harper's lips quirk into a knowing smile.

"It's okay, Alpha. We're all excited to see him," comes Luna's voice from behind them. She practically bounces into the room, her energy as bright as ever, with Jade close behind, her expression more reserved but still present.

Charlotte arches an eyebrow. "Did I wake all of you up?"

Jade shakes her head, dropping onto the couch. "Nah, I was in the gym. Needed to burn off some steam."

Luna moves to the wet bar, nonchalantly pouring herself a glass of wine. "We all needed a break anyway. Besides, if you're pacing holes into the floor, that means something big is on your mind."

Charlotte laughs softly, the weight on her chest loosening slightly, though the tension still lingers. She glances at Harper, then at the rest of them, her pack, her family.

"We like him too, Char," Luna pipes up with a wicked grin. "Plus, I wouldn't mind getting my hands all over that Kai. He's so fucking hot. I bet he could eat my furburger alllll niiiiiight loooooong." She waggles her eyebrows suggestively.

"Damn, Luna. You really don't leave much to the imagination," Jade deadpans, throwing a pillow in her direction.

Luna catches the pillow mid-air, laughing. "Just speaking the truth, babes!"

Before anyone can respond, Isabell appears from around the corner, balancing a tray filled with finger sandwiches, cookies, jerky, and a variety of fruits. "They be hungry, so I make this," she says matter-of-factly, placing the tray on the coffee table.

Charlotte's heart swells with warmth. "Wow, Isabell. That's awesome. You didn't have to do that." She's pretty sure she's falling more in love with the little food angel every day.

Isabell points toward the dining room as she makes her way up the stairs. "They eat there in morning. Breakfast for everyone," she declares before disappearing to her room.

Charlotte glances at the tray, then at her pack. "I swear, we don't deserve her."

Luna laughs, grabbing a sandwich. "You're damn right we don't."

Suddenly, the doorbell rings, the sound obnoxiously loud, and all four women jump up, hearts racing.

Luna bolts to the door first, swinging it open. "Liam!" She throws her arms around his neck without hesitation, catching him completely off guard.

Charlotte chuckles as she watches Liam's eyes go wide, clearly not expecting the ambush.

"Hey, Luna. Did you miss me?" His arms hover awkwardly around her before giving her a few light pats on the back.

Luna pulls away, flashing a mischievous grin. "Nope, just can't wait to kick your ass again." She ducks around him with the agility of a cat, spotting Kai behind him. "Hi, Kai," she teases, wiggling her fingers at him.

Kai waves back, his brows knitting in confusion.

"Luna, let them in before you scare them off," Charlotte calls out, shaking her head, amusement tugging at her lips. "Come on in, everyone. Isabell made some snacks in case you're hungry."

"Starving!" Jaxson steps forward, beaming as he strides past the others. "Hi, Charlotte. Good to see you again, and thanks for letting us crash here."

"Of course," Charlotte replies with a warm smile. "Thanks for coming. It's late, though, so we'll go over the details tomorrow during breakfast."

The rest of the group follows Kai into the great room, leaving just Liam and a young woman who Charlotte assumes must be Maddy. Liam glances back at Charlotte with a soft smile.

"Charlotte, this is my sister, Madeline—Maddy. Maddy, this is my..." He pauses, a hint of hesitation in his voice as he searches for the right words. "Charlotte."

Charlotte steps forward, her smile genuine and welcoming. "Hi, Maddy. Welcome to the Red Rock Den. You're safe here. Our pack has granted both you and Avery full sanctuary and protection."

Maddy looks around the entryway, her eyes wide with awe, much like everyone else when they first walk in. "I can't thank you enough. This place is... incredible."

Charlotte nods. "It's home. And now, it's yours too, for as long as you need."

"Maddy, why don't you go grab a snack? Dinner was a long time ago. Head that way," Liam says, pointing toward the room where the others had disappeared.

As soon as Maddy crosses the threshold, Liam pulls

Charlotte close, pressing her against his chest. His voice drops to a low whisper, full of need. "Fuck, I missed you, woman." He plants a soft kiss on her forehead and inhales deeply, burying his face in her hair. The scent of her grounds him, something raw and primal settling deep in his core.

"I missed you too." Charlotte's fingers curl around the back of his neck, tugging him down as she takes his lips, hard and fast.

He groans into her mouth before pulling back just enough to murmur, "Can we have a slumber party, Red? I promise to let you win at the pillow fight." His eyes stay closed, savoring the closeness.

"Yes, but slumbering isn't in the plans, Nerd." A smirk plays on her lips as she runs her fingers through his hair.

"Good, because I can't stop thinking about how dirty you made me with that dirt meme," he teases, his voice thick with desire.

Charlotte pauses, blinking for a moment before remembering the picture of dirt she'd sent him while he was driving. "I'm glad my dirty meme could sustain you," she replies, sarcasm dripping from every word.

The humor grounds them for a second, but as they walk into the room filled with four unfamiliar males and two women who aren't part of her pack, Charlotte braces herself. Her wolf, usually on edge when strangers are near, stays quiet. The stillness unnerves her. *Are you sleeping? Do you see what I see?*

But as she scans the room, something remarkable catches her off guard. Both packs are mingling, laughing, and easing into a camaraderie that feels... natural. There's no tension, no standoffish posturing. It's almost as if they've always been connected. The air is light, filled with the comfortable sounds of people getting to know each other.

Charlotte feels a flicker of something new. She finds an open chair, sinking into it as she surveys the scene in front of her. The connection between the two groups feels right— too right. For the first time in a long while, she feels a sense of peace, like something has clicked into place. *I'll figure out what this means tomorrow,* she tells herself, but for now, she allows herself to simply be.

BOND OF LIGHT

Charlotte feels Liam's warmth surrounding her, the weight of him like a protective shield. She doesn't move, doesn't open her eyes—just listens to the rhythm of his breaths, steady and calm. It's the calmest she's been in weeks. *How did this happen?*

For years, she'd accepted that love wasn't in the cards for her. She's the Alpha of an all-female pack, and being unwilling to share her territory didn't exactly allow for meeting new wolves. True mates could be found in humans sometimes, sure, but she always knew a human wouldn't be strong enough for her pack, for the complications of her life. But Liam? *Could this really be... love?*

Liam stirs beside her, a soft moan escaping his lips as he pulls her closer. His voice is a rough whisper against her ear. "Good morning, my Queen."

She can't help but smile at the sound of it. "Good morning, indeed. I can't believe you're hard after fucking all night." The curve of his body presses into hers, his arousal a familiar presence against the small of her back.

Liam nuzzles into her neck, his breath warm against her

skin. "That's the power you have over me, Red. One breath of you, and I'm ready." His hand glides from her hip, slipping between her legs, fingers finding their target with practiced ease. "And look at you—you're just as ready as I am."

Her body responds before her mind even catches up, legs parting to give him access. The soreness from their marathon night of passion lingers—memories of the shower, the bathroom floor, bent over the counter, sprawled on the bedroom floor, and finally the bed. But it's a good kind of ache, one she wouldn't trade for anything. *If it weren't for family breakfast...*

"Fuck, your pussy is so incredible," he murmurs, his voice thick with awe. His fingers move with a rhythm that has her melting, teasing the bundle of nerves that only he seems to know how to reach. "You're my fantasy, Charlotte. Everything I've ever wanted."

Her body reacts instantly, every touch sending waves of bliss crashing through her. Liam knows her—every inch of her. It's like he's memorized the map of her body, found every road to pleasure she didn't even know existed.

Liam's voice drips with heat, sending a wave of sensation through her. "I love how wet you are." His breath hitches, his tone thick with desire. "Fuck, Charlotte. Moan again. That's it. Thank you for telling me I'm doing right by you."

His teeth graze the curve of her neck, a sharp bite that pulls a whimper from deep inside her. She can't hold it back, not with the way his words and touch wrap around her.

"Yes, Charlotte. Make all the sounds. I don't need words."

Reaching down, she grabs his hand, and slides it lower, guiding his fingers inside her, intertwining her own with his.

The moment his fingers press into her, she feels his body tense, his cock grinding harder against her back.

"Fuck yeah, Charlotte," he growls, the heat of his body pushing into hers. Their movements sync perfectly, her back arching to give him more, her hips rolling to match his rhythm.

"I'm going to come, Charlotte," his breath hitches, voice ragged, his body trembling with restraint as he thrusts harder against her.

"Come with me, Liam," she whispers, the words laced with both command and need.

With a sudden move, his arms wrap around her waist, flipping her onto her back effortlessly. He straddles her hips, his gaze dark and possessive. "Put those fingers back in your pussy, Red. We aren't done yet." His hand strokes his cock, his thumb sweeping over the tip, drawing her gaze. "I'm going to put my scent all over you. I want everyone to know I'm yours."

The sight of him—his strong hand moving over his length, the tension in his body—is enough to set her on fire. She arches her back, the heat inside her building, and then she's lost in it, her entire body shaking with the force of her climax. "Liam..." It's the only word she manages before she feels him release, warmth splattering across her chest in hot bursts. Her wolf practically rolls in the sensation, reveling in the fact that he's marked her, that he's claimed her in a way that goes beyond the physical.

As she lies there, chest rising and falling, she looks up at him—his beautifully chiseled abs, the sheen of sweat on his skin, his golden eyes glowing with the intensity of his wolf. She feels a new sense of pride, a bond she didn't expect but welcomes.

"Fuck, Nerd," she breathes, still catching her breath, her hand resting between her legs. "I hope you like the desert."

Liam leans down, his hands bracing on either side of her head, his lips curling into a grin. "Why's that?"

"I don't think I can live without these orgasms anymore." She smirks, the playful tease masking the weight of what's really happening between them.

His eyes darken, his wolf hovering just beneath the surface. "Charlotte... I love the desert."

After quickly showering, they run downstairs where everyone has already sat down to breakfast. Who knew the table was going to come in this handy someday? The Lazy Susan is in full motion while everyone fills their plates with pancakes, bacon, eggs, sausage, biscuits, and gravy. "Wow, she forgot nothing, did she?" Charlotte says while grabbing her plate and stabbing a piece of ham.

"Out of all the things here, I don't see chorizo. That

doesn't even make sense." Jade yells towards the kitchen. "Isabell? Why no chorizo?"

From the kitchen we hear, "Open you eye. Chorizo there!"

"I've got it." Jaxson spins the tray.

It takes a few minutes for everyone to fill their plates. The silence tells Charlotte that the Humboldt's appreciate Isabell's food as much as they do.

"Everyone sleep ok?" Charlotte asks uncomfortably. She knows she isn't the best host, but since they are here, she had better try.

"Oh yeah. I don't know what you ladies do for work, but this house is amazing. What are those fucking beds made of... clouds? I slept like a newborn baby." Spencer says, chewing down his food.

"Thanks. This bitch is a lot, but our pack is expanding, and this gives us the room needed." She looks over at Maddy and gives her a wink. "Plus, sometimes when something feels right," Charlotte lifts one shoulder slightly, "you just have to follow that yellow brick road."

Charlotte looks around the table while the group continues to chat and fill up on Isabell's breakfast. Luna and Harper are fighting over the last sausage patty while Liam and Jade are talking about his Bronco. She needs to process this feeling. Is it happiness? Whatever it is, she could get addicted to it.

With full bellies, they all move to the game room. Jaxson and Jade are at the pool table while the others get comfy on the couch and fluffy chairs.

Spencer had pulled Charlotte aside last night before everyone went to bed to apologize again. Of course, no apologies were necessary. They talk about how fate seems to have woken up because they have big changes in both their packs' futures. She was thankful for their alliance and looked forward to many more gatherings in the future. They both agreed to partake in an old custom, of binding the two packs together.

Charlotte looks around the room for Liam. She realizes that he has taken a sentinel stance behind her. She knows she doesn't need a protector, but damnit if it didn't feel good to know he's there.

"First, I want to thank the Humboldt's for going and rescuing Avery and Maddy. They went into another's territory based on my word alone. That trust will never be forgotten. Second, Thank you for creating an alliance between our packs. Ladies, we have fought hard, and our losses are felt every day. But keeping the city safe from outsiders has become more than the four of us can handle." Charlotte leans over, grabbing the small dagger that was resting on the top of the chess table.

"Spencer as a symbol of my allegiance to the Humboldt Pack until your death," She swipes the dagger across her palm. "I give you the blood of the Red Rock Alpha"

Standing tall, Spencer strides to Charlotte. He takes the dagger and runs it across his palm. They lock fists to wrists. Charlotte learned the importance of the Blood Oath while with the Black Canyon pack. Covering the wrist with your blood is a symbol of your fealty. You will give your blood to protect their weak spot.

"I give you the blood of the Humboldt Alpha," Spencer locks eyes with her.

Harper steps forward next, her face resolute as she takes the blade and grips Spencer's wrist, locking eyes with him as she pledges her loyalty. One by one, the members of both packs follow suit, sealing the alliance in blood. All but Liam. His stance, unchanged, his eyes tracking every movement with the sharpness of a hawk. The intensity rolling off him is palpable, like electricity waiting for a storm.

Charlotte feels it—his quiet power, his unwavering gaze burning into her soul. When Jaxson, the last to pledge, is done and the dagger is set down once again on the chess table, there's a moment of stillness. Silence. Then Liam moves.

Without a word, he strides to the front of the room, stepping before Charlotte with purpose. His eyes drop to the floor as he picks up the dagger, and suddenly, everything feels different. He lowers himself to one knee, his head still bowed. "Charlotte Randolph, Alpha of the Red Rock Pack," he says, his voice raw, unguarded. "I am a lone wolf, pledged to no Alpha."

He slides the blade across his wrist, the cut deep enough to bleed, a line of crimson pooling against his skin. "I give you my blood. This body is yours to command, my queen. I will protect you, your lands, and your pack. I give you my fealty."

Charlotte feels her breath catch in her throat. She's been through battle, through loss, through leadership, but nothing has prepared her for this. The room feels heavy with the weight of what's happening, and the tears she's been holding back finally fall. She can barely speak as she reaches down, taking the dagger from his hand with trembling fingers.

"Please stand, Liam," she whispers, her voice thick with emotion. She pulls him up, forcing him to look her in the eyes. His gaze is unwavering, intense, as though he's offering not just his loyalty but his soul. "I accept your fealty, Liam Dunne." She draws the blade across her own wrist, a matching wound to his, and holds her arm out.

Liam presses his bleeding wrist against hers, their blood

mingling in the air between them, and in that instant, everything changes.

A burst of energy—unlike anything Charlotte has ever felt—surges through her, radiating from the place where their blood meets. It slams into her with such force that her knees nearly buckle. Her vision goes white, and for a moment, nothing else exists. The room fades away, leaving only golden light, warm and pure, surrounding them like a protective cocoon. The energy between them pulses, growing larger, stronger, until it feels as if it's filling every corner of her being.

Her breath catches again, but this time it's not from shock—it's from a deep, bone-deep understanding. She and Liam aren't just connected by blood now; they're bound by something far more powerful. Something that feels ancient and eternal. His eyes stay locked on hers, and she knows he feels it too. This is more than an oath. More than loyalty. This is a bond that defies every law of nature, every rule of their world.

When the golden light finally fades, Charlotte blinks, shaking her head as if to clear it. She glances around, suddenly aware that the room has gone eerily silent. Everyone is staring, wide-eyed.

"Holy shit," she mutters under her breath. She looks around at the faces of her pack, then back at Liam, whose gaze is as intense as ever.

"Char," Harper's voice comes from beside her, and then Charlotte feels a sharp pinch on her arm.

"Ow! What the hell, Harper?" she snaps, rubbing her arm.

"I had to make sure you were real." Harper takes a step back, her eyes still wide. "Char... you turned into light. Like, actual light."

"What?" Charlotte's brow furrows as she looks from Harper to the rest of her pack. They're all staring at her as if they've just seen a ghost.

Jade speaks up, her voice filled with awe. "She's right, Alpha. You and Liam—your bodies were outlined, but you were glowing. Pure light. It only lasted a second, but damn, it was incredible."

Liam's chest is heaving, his eyes flicking between his wrist and Charlotte's. "I feel...in-fucking-credible." His voice is low, but it vibrates with something primal, something ancient. "Red, do you feel different? Do you feel more... powerful?"

Charlotte takes a breath, and the energy still crackling inside her feels like it's running through her veins like fire. "Yeah... I feel it. My body is buzzing, like I've got lightning running through me."

Luna's voice cuts through the tension, her excitement barely contained. "Oh my god! You found your true mate! I've read about this! It's rare, but it's called 'The Bond of Light.'" She rushes to Charlotte, practically bouncing with excitement. "It's the strongest bond in existence. The old texts say you can even heal."

Charlotte frowns. "We've always been able to heal, Luna. That's not new."

Luna shakes her head, her phone already out as she scrolls furiously. "No, no, not just yourselves, Alpha. You and Liam might be able to heal others now. It's a gift that only a light bond can give—when it's strong enough."

Charlotte feels Liam's hand tighten around hers, and she looks up at him. His eyes are glowing with that golden light, the one that tells her his wolf is right there, just beneath the surface.

"Charlotte... I love you," he says, the words falling from

his lips like a confession, raw and unfiltered. There's no hesitation in his voice, no doubt in his gaze. Just certainty.

And in that moment, Charlotte knows that whatever comes next, whatever battle or war they face, they're in this together. Forever.

"Okay, well... let's hope we never have to test that," Charlotte says, her voice steady, but the weight of what just happened is still heavy on her chest. She exhales deeply, trying to shake off the surreal feeling that lingers in the air. "That took an unexpected turn." From her seat, she surveys the room, noticing how everyone's eyes have finally returned to their normal size, the awe starting to fade.

Behind her, Liam moves closer, his presence like a warm shadow. He leans down, his lips brushing her ear as his voice drops low, filled with a playful edge. "Now you're stuck with me, Red." She doesn't have to see his face to know he's smiling.

The intimate moment is interrupted as Isabell walks in with Jase trailing behind her. Jase stops abruptly, eyes wide as he takes in the scene, his usual cocky grin faltering. "Whoa! This meeting's a bit more cozy than I expected." He glances between Charlotte and Liam, brows raised.

"Jase," Charlotte says, straightening herself, "this is Spencer, Lucas, Kai, and Jaxson of the Humboldt Pack out of Oregon. Avery and Maddy are now under Red Rock protection," she gestures to the two women, "and this is Liam Dunne, the lone wolf you asked about."

Everyone either nods, waves, or grunts in Jase's direction as he surveys the room.

"Jase Hansen," Charlotte continues, "is our extremely annoying regional COPS Enforcer. I asked him here because I thought it was a good idea to read him in on the plan. We don't need anything coming back to bite the Red Rocks—or Humboldt—in the ass."

Jase chuckles at the introduction but doesn't interrupt. He leans casually against the doorframe, arms crossed, watching.

She looks around the room, her gaze locking with each person as she begins to lay out the plan. "The goal is to make this look real enough to draw the Cascades into the warehouse, but we stay in control of the situation at all times. Spencer, you and your team will be outside, ready to guide them in when the time comes. If anything feels off, we regroup immediately—no hero moves. I want everyone to stay safe."

Charlotte pauses, her gaze narrowing as she adds, "And we can't forget about this powder shit. We don't know if Miles has more of it or how he plans to use it. That stuff is fucking ridiculous and I don't want anyone taking chances. If you see anything suspicious—anything at all—you call it out. Understood?"

A murmur of agreement ripples through the room, but the mention of the powder creates tension and unspoken fears hang in the air like a storm cloud.

"Any questions so far?" she asks, her voice steady despite the weight pressing down on her.

Before Charlotte can move on, a sharp jolt shatters the pack bond, stealing the breath from her lungs. Her eyes snap to Luna just as the smaller sister stiffens, her body jerking violently.

"Luna!" Kai growls, moving with a speed that defies reason. He catches her as she starts to collapse, his arms wrapping around her like a shield. Panic flares in his usually jovial eyes as he cradles her trembling body.

The room erupts into chaos. Chairs scrape the floor, voices rise in confusion, and Charlotte's wolf claws against her chest, desperate to act.

"Give her space!" Jase's sharp command slices through the noise like a blade. He strides forward, his expression unusually serious as he kneels beside Luna. "It's a seizure," he says, his tone calm but firm. "Lay her flat—gently. She needs to ride it out. Don't hold her down."

Kai's growl deepens, low and threatening. His arms tighten protectively around Luna, his narrowed eyes burning into Jase like a warning.

"She's safe with me," Kai snaps, his voice a raw growl.

Jase meets his gaze head-on, unflinching. "This isn't about trust. It's about her. If you care for her, do as I say."

Charlotte watches as the tension crackles between them, thick and electric. Her wolf bristles, ready to step in and kick both their asses, but Kai exhales through clenched teeth. With deliberate care, he lowers Luna's still-trembling body to the floor, his movements slow and hesitant. His hand lingers on her shoulder, his thumb brushing against her skin—a silent promise that he's staying right by her side.

Jase watches him, his expression unreadable. He reaches out, brushing a strand of hair away from Luna's forehead, his touch surprisingly gentle. "Easy now," he murmurs, his voice steady and calm. "She's strong—she'll get through this." His hand moves briefly to Kai's, resting there for just a heartbeat. The gesture is subtle, almost imperceptible, but it carries weight—an unspoken connection that lingers in the air like a question begging for answers.

Charlotte watches the exchange, her instincts flaring. There's something deeper between these two men, an unspoken understanding tied to Luna, fragile but undeniable. She files the thought away, focusing instead on Luna as the tremors begin to subside.

The room falls silent except for Luna's slowing breaths. When her body finally stills, Jase leans back, his usual smirk absent. His gaze flicks briefly to Kai, then returns to Luna, his expression shadowed by something Charlotte can't name.

"She's out of immediate danger," Jase says quietly, rising to his feet. His voice carries no triumph, only weariness. "But this isn't random. That powder you mentioned—it's not just dangerous. It's targeted."

Charlotte's wolf bristles at his words, her instincts screaming for answers. "How the hell do you know that?" she demands, suspicion sharpening her tone.

Jase doesn't meet her eyes, his focus fixed on Luna's pale face. "Just trust me," he mutters, jaw tight.

The pack exchanges uneasy glances, the weight of unspoken questions pressing down on the room: *What the hell is this shit?*

Kai shifts closer to Luna, his protective stance unwavering, as if daring anyone—even Jase—to come near her. Jase steps back slowly, his gaze lingering on Luna longer than necessary. There's something unreadable in his expression, something dark and calculated that sends a shiver through Charlotte's wolf.

The tension between Jase and Kai simmers, their shared protectiveness over Luna feeling less like teamwork and more like a battle for dominance.

Charlotte swallows hard, her instincts clawing at her. This wasn't just a random episode, and her gut screams that Jase knows more than he's letting on. The way his eyes narrow, the slight smirk tugging at his lips as he leans against the doorframe—it's not just confidence. It's something more dangerous.

Miles and his powder linger in her mind, but now another question takes root: *What the hell is Jase really after?*

THINGS ARE NOT ALWAYS
WHAT THEY SEEM

The fake "Grand Opening" has finally arrived. For the past week, Luna's hacker skills had unleashed a cyberstorm on the Cascades, plastering the internet with "Come Check Out the Hottest New Gym in Vegas" ads. Aimed directly at Miles, it ensured he knew it was Charlotte's gym—and more importantly—that all four of the Red Rocks would be there, waiting.

Standing in the center of the empty warehouse, Charlotte's wolf thrums with anticipation, claws itching to shift beneath her skin. Her heightened senses catch every creak, every faint breath of air that stirs the dust on the concrete floor. The space is small, just enough to hold a fight but not enough to escape easily. It's perfect.

Outside, Spencer and the rest of his pack blend in with the few random people pretending to be new gym clients. Avery and Maddy, disguised as employees, are stationed at the entrance, primed for the role they're playing in this deadly theater. Vegas is convenient like that—outdoor gyms were trending. They didn't even need to fabricate an entire indoor facility. Just enough to sell the illusion.

Behind her, Harper, Jade, and Luna stand quietly, a wall of strength and shared purpose. Charlotte can feel the fierce determination crackling between them through the bond, their readiness for battle pulsing in time with her own. No words are needed. Their vehemence, their thirst for justice, is a tangible thing.

Then, the moment arrives.

"They're here." Liam's text buzzes against her hip. The message is short, but it's all she needs.

Charlotte rolls her neck again, feeling the last knot of tension release with a satisfying pop. Tossing her phone onto the chair off to the side, she locks in. It's time. No turning back now.

The door creaks open, and the sound is louder than it should be, echoing in the empty space. One by one, five men file in. All tall. All muscular. The air grows thick, weighted with the tension of what's about to unfold. Her wolf prowls beneath the surface, hackles raised.

Her gaze zeroes in on the third man through the door—Miles.

He's limping. *Good.*

The shock that crosses his face when he spots her standing there is better than she imagined. His mix of disbelief and simmering anger—it's delicious. Her wolf preens, practically purring with satisfaction at the power shift in the room. For the first time in too long, she's not on the defensive. Seeing the flicker of doubt shadow his eyes sends a euphoric surge through her veins. He wasn't expecting this. He wasn't expecting *her*.

"Oh, look," Charlotte mutters under her breath, loud enough for him to catch. "He's surprised. Isn't this fun?"

"Oh, Charlotte." Miles's voice drips with condescension as he surveys the empty warehouse, still trying to cling to control. "This is cute. Did you draw us here to fight?" He smirks, but it's weak, his gaze sweeping the room with a thinly veiled disdain. He's trying too hard to appear unaffected. Charlotte feels her wolf stir, the urge to bare her teeth almost overwhelming.

But she reins it in, opting instead for a different approach. A slow smile curls her lips as she places a hand over her chest, feigning innocence with an exaggerated gesture. "My? Whatever are you talking about, Miles?" Her voice is sickening sweet, sarcasm dripping from each word. "We're just testing out our *new outdoor gym*."

Her eyes narrow slightly, calculating. Inside, her wolf paces, restless. Her pack bristles behind her, their emotions humming through the bond like electricity in the air. Harper's presence is a steady pulse of controlled rage at her back. The others are ready too, just waiting for her signal.

She watches as Miles's eyes flicker, scanning the space, doubt creeping in despite himself. He's not sure what's happening. And that's exactly where she wants him.

Good.

They want him rattled, just enough to tip him off balance. Not too much—*not yet*. Let him think, just for a moment, that he still has the upper hand. It'll make the fall that much sweeter.

Without warning, Luna moves, padding past Charlotte with the casual grace of a predator that knows it owns the room. She stops inches from Miles, looking up at him through narrowed eyes, rising onto her tiptoes until they're nose to nose.

"We would never *draw* you here," she sneers, voice low and dripping venom. "We fucking *hate* you, you wet sock."

Miles snickers, his lips curling into a smug grin as he throws a glance over his shoulder at the other nefarious assholes flanking him. The movement is slow, deliberate, as if he's drawing confidence from their presence, a silent reassurance that he's untouchable. His eyes flick back to Luna, amusement dancing behind them, his posture relaxed as though the threat she poses is laughable.

For a brief second, his smirk grows wider, a half-scoff escaping his throat, as if she's just a pesky insect buzzing too close. He shifts his weight slightly, settling into a cocky stance, his body language practically screaming *I'm not afraid of you.*

Charlotte can feel all her wolves are ready, including Maddy, who has an unexpected confidence. The Humboldt's have now snuck in behind the oblivious idiots. *They aren't even good at being werewolves.*

Luna steps back, just enough to shift her focus from Miles to Ethan, her gaze sharp and unflinching. She must be striking a nerve, because Ethan's wolf begins to surface, sharing his face with a fury that's barely restrained. His eyes glow with a dangerous intensity, the subtle twitch in his jaw betraying his struggle to keep the beast at bay.

Luna's lips curve into a sly smile, knowing exactly what buttons she's pressing. She holds his gaze, unbothered by the darkening shift in his features, as if daring him to lose control. "Come. Come Luna. However, will you bow to me with that attitude?"

The door closing over her shoulder shakes Luna out of her death stare with Ethan. Her eyes slowly move back to Miles. She bumps his chest, and turns on her heel, giving her back to the enemy... one of the biggest insults you can give in the shifter world.

Damn, that girl knows how to fuck with people. Charlotte can feel Liam take a seat behind her, giving her the signal that the biggest piece of the plan is now set in place.

"We've had enough of war with you, Miles. This is the last time we will *pretty please* ask you to leave Vegas alone. The four of us came here because nobody wanted this dust ball. We made it ours and it will stay that way."

"Things change, Red Rock Alpha. We offered to share the city with you, but Ethan tells me you turned down my generous offer, so now we'll take it by force. I challenge you, Charlotte."

The words hang in the air, a clear, deliberate threat, and before Charlotte can respond, Miles begins his shift. It's fast —unnervingly so. His bones crack with a sickening snap, his muscles contorting and elongating with a swiftness that sends a ripple of energy through the room. Fur erupts along his skin, dark and bristling, and his eyes glow with primal fury as his human form dissolves into the hulking shape of a grey wolf.

With a powerful howl, his four paws slam onto the floor, the sound reverberating through the space like thunder. His chest heaves with barely held aggression, claws digging into the ground, ready for battle. The transformation is seamless, as though the wolf has always been lying just beneath the surface, waiting to burst free.

Charlotte's heart pounds, but her stance stays firm, her eyes locked on Miles. He's fast, she'll give him that. But she's smarter.

Her wolf stirs beneath her skin, itching to break free, but Charlotte holds back, the anticipation buzzing in her veins. A grin tugs at her lips just as the crack of a dart gun rings out behind her. Miles' wolf staggers, his large body swaying left, then right. He stumbles forward a few steps, disoriented, before his face slams into the floor with a satisfying thud.

What a fucking glorious sound.

"What the fuck?" Ethan's voice slices through the air, his shock palpable as he stares down at his fallen Alpha. The other goons are frozen, heads swiveling between Miles and Charlotte, clearly unsure of what to do. Eli, ever the coward, starts to back away, his retreat slow and careful.

But his escape is short-lived. He collides into a wall—except it's not a wall. It's Spencer. Eli may be average for a wolf shifter, but Spencer towers over him by half a foot. And while Spencer is usually the calm one, today the war dog is out, and his presence radiates raw power. Eli barely dares to breathe.

Charlotte hasn't budged, her arms still crossed, the smirk on her lips growing. "Thanks, Jase."

Jase is already crouched down, cuffing a—now—in human form, unconscious Miles. The effects of the dart are still keeping him out cold. "Cascade Pack, your Alpha is being detained for unlawful shifting," Jase announces, his voice authoritative, cutting through any possible objections.

Ethan's face twists with anger, his voice climbing higher with frustration. "It's only illegal to shift in front of humans!"

Charlotte's grin widens, enjoying the spectacle. "You might want to check your facts, Ethan. You're not as clever as you think."

Jase gestures behind Charlotte, where Liam and Isabell are standing. "And Miles Barlowe did, in fact, shift in front of a human."

Ethan's fury boils over. "You bitch!" He lunges at Charlotte, his movements wild with rage. But she easily steps out of his path, sending him sliding headfirst into Jade's shoes.

"Oopsy. You fell. Need a hand?" Jade offers her hand with a mocking smile.

Ethan slaps her hand away, scrambling to his feet. "This isn't over, Red Rocks."

Charlotte tips her head, the challenge clear in her eyes. "Oh? Is that a threat, Ethan?"

Seething, Ethan stomps toward the door but stops short, glaring at Lucas, who is still blocking part of the exit. His voice is venomous. "We let you into our pack. We trusted you. We won't forget this betrayal, Williams."

Lucas stands firm, saying nothing, his face unreadable as he sidesteps to allow Ethan and the rest of the goons to pass. The door slams against the wall with such force that the glass shatters, a sharp crack echoing through the room.

"I think they're pissed," Lucas remarks, casually tugging his hoodie up over his head, as if the chaos hadn't touched him at all.

Charlotte scans the room, her eyes sweeping over her pack. "Everyone good?"

Liam and Jase are lifting a still-drooling Miles off the floor. "We're going to go put this asshole in my truck," Jase grunts, straining under the weight.

"Holy shit, Alpha," Jade grins wide, clearly proud of herself. "An idea of mine didn't end in blood. Who fucking knew I had it in me?"

Luna bolts over like a flying squirrel, launching herself into Jade's arms. "I didn't have to let the beast out. Thanks, Jade!"

"Sure, Nugget. I got you." Jade throws her arms around her much smaller friend in a mock-squeeze.

Charlotte walks to the back of the small warehouse locking eyes with Isabell. "You good? Did that scare you?"

"Oh, no, señora. I see it before." Isabell shakes her head, calm as ever. "It no bother me."

Charlotte places a hand on her shoulder. "Thank you for coming. You saved lives today."

"Hey, Williams!" Harper's voice cuts through. "Wanna get pizza and fuck?"

Lucas doesn't miss a beat, striding toward her in large steps. "Yes, but I hope you like cold pizza." With a wink, he scoops Harper up by the waist, spinning her effortlessly.

"Pizza sounds great!" Jaxson claps his hands, already halfway out the door. "Did I hear we're getting pizza?"

"Jaxson, are you ever *not* hungry?" Harper asks, perched on Lucas' hips.

Kai, Spencer, Lucas, and Isabell all reply in unison, "No."

"Isabell?" Charlotte raises an eyebrow, a deep crease forming on her forehead.

"What?" Isabell shrugs. "I never leave kitchen since he come to house."

Jaxson, with no shame, saunters toward the door. "It's her fault. Her damn food is incredible, and we have great conversations."

Spencer chimes in, "I saw a billboard for a pizza place, one exit back. Charlotte's buying."

Charlotte chuckles, hands on her hips. "Fair enough, but only if you help bring that gym equipment in here first." She points at the door, a playful glint in her eye.

THE GROTTO

The pizza place Jaxson picked was superb, but Charlotte learned the hard way that large shifter men can really put the food away. Five hundred dollars later, she's lounging in a blue chair by the pool, sipping on some type of fruity concoction Spencer whipped up. Her drink's sweetness is matched only by the chaos unfolding in front of her.

Jaxson cannonballs into the pool, sending a wave crashing over the edge. Lucas and Harper sway to the music filling the backyard. Their connection palpable, as Harper hums along to the music.

"This song is too slow," DJ Jade complains from her spot near the speaker, arms crossed like a petulant teenager.

"Stop bitching," Harper snaps, her movements never faltering. "Hozier has the sexiest music on the planet."

Before Jade can retort, Kai's voice booms from the peak of the grotto mountain. "I must find my beauty!" He's pounding his chest like a deranged King Kong, the moonlight glinting off his wet skin.

"I'm here!" Luna shouts from the far end of the pool, waving dramatically. "Save me, Kong!"

"Ew, are we watching their roleplay?" Jade's voice cuts through the backyard, dripping with mock disgust as the music cuts off. "Someone get me a blindfold. I'm going to need therapy after this."

Kai splashes dramatically, sending another wave cascading over the edge of the pool. "Don't be jealous, Jade. Some people can appreciate a good performance."

"Performance?" Jade scoffs, crossing her arms. "That was more like bad improv night at a rundown theater."

Charlotte snorts, wiping more water from her face. "Come on, man. Take your foreplay to her hot tub or something."

From her left, Liam leans casually against the edge of the pool, clicking his tongue against his cheek. His grin is pure trouble. "Can I take my foreplay to your hot tub, Red?"

Charlotte narrows her eyes at him, the corner of her lips twitching despite herself. "Keep talking like that, and you'll be sleeping in it tonight."

The pack dissolves into laughter, the sounds echoing into the night. For a brief moment, the world feels lighter— no enemies, no threats, just the simple joy of being together.

Charlotte rises slowly, peeling off the turquoise wrap from her waist, letting it fall to the ground. She knows Liam is watching her every move, the air between them thick with unspoken desire. She turns her head slightly, catching his gaze. "I have a better idea," she says softly, feeling the weight of the moment. She walks toward the grotto, her steps slow and deliberate, every nerve buzzing with anticipation. When she ducks behind the rock wall, her heart races.

She hears the splash of water and knows he's following. A small smile tugs at her lips. *Good.* He surfaces right in front of her, droplets running down his face, his eyes locked on hers.

"Did you notice Isabell called you *Señora* earlier?" His voice is a quiet rumble, sending shivers down her spine.

"Yes, I did." She hesitates, surprised by her own honesty. "I have to admit, I sort of liked it."

"Sort of?" Liam leans in, brushing his lips over her nose, so tender it makes her chest ache.

"Okay, I liked it," she admits, feeling exposed in more ways than one. "It feels strange, but right. Like it was meant to be."

"Yeah, I feel that too," he murmurs, his hand reaching up to cup her breast, his touch igniting her skin. "But right now, all I want is to feel your body against mine."

Her pulse quickens, but she steps back, teasing him, leading him deeper into the grotto. The glowing lights reflecting off the water cast shadows that dance across their bodies. She knows he's following, thinks he's still in control, but that's about to change.

When her back touches the wall, she pivots, spinning him around so that his back hits the stone. He looks at her, surprise flashing across his face, but she doesn't give him time to react. Grabbing his wrist, she lifts it above his head and secures it in the cuff before he realizes what's happening.

"Holy shit, Red," he laughs, looking up at the cuff on his wrist. "Cuffs in the grotto? Unexpected." His eyes darken with curiosity. "What about the other one?"

"I need that too," she purrs, taking his other wrist and binding it with a firm but gentle touch. Her heart pounds as she steps back, drinking him in—Liam, completely vulnerable, completely hers.

She moves toward him again, her hands sliding over his

chest, feeling the hard muscles beneath her fingertips. Her eyes fall on the tribal butterfly tattoo. "Why a tribal butterfly?" she asks softly, tracing the ink.

"I got it after Sophie died," he admits, his voice quieter now. "She loved butterflies."

A pang of emotion hits her, but she doesn't pull away. Instead, she lets her hands roam over his body, feeling every inch of him. "Liam, don't worry about talking about Sophie. She's a part of you, and that means I care about her too. One day, I'd like to know more about her. But right now..." Her hand slides down to his cock, already hard in her grip. "Right now, I'm going to learn everything about you."

A deep moan escapes him, his hips instinctively bucking into her hand as she strokes him. The sound of the chains rattling fills the grotto as he tugs against the restraints, his desire palpable. "Fuck, I don't know if I like this," he mutters, his breathing uneven.

"You will," she promises, leaning in, her tongue tracing a line from his navel up to his chest, savoring the way his body responds to her touch. She can feel the heat of him, the tension in his muscles as he tries to keep control.

"What if someone comes in?" he asks, his voice strained but teasing.

"Then they'll see how a queen takes care of her king." She squeezes his cock, her words sending a jolt of pleasure through him. His body twitches, and she feels his arousal throb in her hand. "You liked that, didn't you?"

"I liked being called your king," he groans, his voice a raw mix of lust and adoration. "But I won't be able to hold you, fuck you properly, if I'm cuffed like this."

"That's the point," she whispers, pressing her body closer, letting him feel her warmth against him. "You have no control right now. You're mine to play with. Later, in bed, you can have your turn."

Her other hand cups his balls, squeezing gently, drawing another deep moan from his lips. His body trembles beneath her touch. "Fuck, Charlotte. You always keep me guessing."

She quickens her pace, watching every flicker of pleasure cross his face. This moment is hers—her control, her trust, her release. "Liam, tell me one of your fantasies," she breathes, biting his chest gently, her strokes growing more insistent.

"Fuck, Red," he groans, his voice ragged, his body straining against the cuffs. "This. With you. Always you." His words are broken, each one coming out between labored breaths.

"Does it feel good, Liam?" she whispers, her lips brushing his ear as her hand works him. "Do you like how my hand feels around your cock?"

"Yes. Fuck, Charlotte, don't stop. Please... fuck... I'm going to come," he gasps, his body shaking with the force of his release. "Jesus, I'm going to—"

His moan fills the grotto as his orgasm takes over, his body convulsing in her hands, completely undone. She watches him, breathless, overwhelmed by the sight of him, by the power of what they've shared.

Gently, she reaches up and releases one of the cuffs. As soon as his hand is free, he cups her chin, lifting her face to meet his gaze. His eyes are filled with something she's never seen before—complete surrender, complete love. "You... are... my queen," he whispers, his voice hoarse but full of emotion.

The weight of his words crashes over her, flooding her with emotions she thought she had buried long ago. She never thought she'd want or need this—someone who could see through her armor and love her for all that she was. But now, in Liam's arms, she knows she does. She can't imagine life without him by her side.

Her lips meet his again, the kiss deep and consuming. For the first time in so many years, she feels safe, loved, and supported. This is everything she thought she'd sacrificed to become queen of the desert.

As the kiss breaks, Liam's breath mingles with hers, and he whispers, "You never have to be alone again, Charlotte. I'm here. Eternal."

Her heart swells, and she pulls back just enough to meet his eyes, her voice steady but filled with raw emotion. "I know. And I' am yours."

OK, FINE THE ENEMY OF
MY ENEMY IS MY FRIEND

The next morning, Charlotte meanders into the dining room, her messy bun flopping atop her head, eyes half-open. The familiar sound of laughter and clinking plates greets her as the packs, once again, fill the room, shoveling food into their mouths like they haven't eaten in days.

"Good god," she groans, sliding into her chair and reaching for the coffee carafe. "Doesn't anyone else sleep around here?"

Luna, grinning with mischief, throws a biscuit across the table. "Sleep? Is that what you call it? I don't remember you crying 'Oh god, yes. Right there,' in your sleep before."

Charlotte catches the biscuit without even looking, a smirk on her lips.

But Jade, wide-eyed and mock-offended, pipes up. "You're one to talk! 'Oh Kai, eat it, Daddy. Yeah, like that!'" She throws her hands up in exasperation. "I swear I'm the only one not getting laid in this house."

"I could fix that," Jaxson mumbles with indifference around a mouthful of pancake.

"Nah, not feeling it, man," Jade shrugs, though there's a playful glint in her eye.

"Your loss," Jaxson mutters, already digging into another bite.

The teasing dies down as Spencer stabs at a Polish sausage on his plate, his expression shifting slightly. "We'll be heading out after breakfast," he says, his tone tinged with a certain heaviness. "Not getting Isabell's food every day is going to be the biggest regret of my life."

"The Humboldts are welcome in our den anytime," Charlotte says, her tone sincere as she sets down her coffee. She can feel the shift in the air—their time together winding down, the inevitable parting drawing closer.

Spencer nods, though his gaze drifts to the glass doors leading to the garden, where Maddy and Avery are talking. His face softens, a flicker of uncertainty crossing his features. "I'm not sure yet if Avery's coming with me," he admits quietly, almost to himself, his eyes never leaving the door.

The tension in the room becomes more noticeable as Charlotte watches the interaction between Lucas and Harper. Lucas, unusually quiet, catches Charlotte's eye. His hand is entwined with Harper's beneath the table, and while neither of them speaks, the weight of their emotions is undeniable. It's the kind of sadness that comes when bonds are formed quickly but have to stretch across miles.

Charlotte's wolf stirs, unsettled, feeling the weight of the impending goodbyes. The tug of the pack bond pulls at her heart, something instinctual, a desire to keep those she's grown close to, nearby. The packs have become more than allies. They've become intertwined, and the parting feels like the slow unraveling of something that had only just come together.

Her wolf feels the loss keenly, bristling at the thought of separation. *This is the way of packs,* she reminds herself. They come together, they part ways, but the bonds remain. The logic of it doesn't make it easier.

She glances at Lucas and Harper again, their quiet connection reflecting the sadness she feels. They've shared laughter, fights, and now an unspoken grief that hangs in the air. Charlotte's heart aches, her wolf restless, but she pushes it down. There's no stopping this part of life.

With a deep breath, she takes a sip of her coffee, savoring these final moments together. The whoosh of the door grabs her attention as Maddy and Avery step inside.

"I am," Avery says, her voice louder than usual but still soft, as she stands in the doorway. The shy smile on her face says it all—Avery's made her decision.

Maddy steps in behind her, concern etched into her features, her protective stance unmistakable. Charlotte recognizes the look, that fierce protectiveness of a she-wolf guarding her pack.

Spencer's reaction is immediate. "Yes!" He jumps up from his chair, his joy filling the room as he practically barrels toward Avery. In a blink, she's swept into his arms, her face disappearing into his chest as he hugs her tightly, his chin resting on her head. "We're a bunch of backwoods brutes, but I'll do everything in my power to make you happy," he murmurs, his voice rough with emotion.

Avery's giggle, muffled against his chest, is soft but unmistakably happy. Charlotte watches, her own emotions swirling as she takes in the scene.

Adorable, she thinks, watching Spencer's unguarded happiness and Avery's shy acceptance. Her heart twinges unexpectedly. *This love shit is making me soft.*

Liam comes around the side of the table, burying his

face in the crock of her neck, then a little nip before whispering, "Eat up, you'll need your strength later." Ok, maybe the love shit ain't so bad. Charlotte cannot help the giggle that escapes her as well.

After devouring more pancakes than IHOP probably makes in a day, Spencer, Kai, and Lucas say their goodbyes to Isabell, their voices warm but tinged with the sadness of parting. They make their way toward the foyer, laughter still lingering in the air as they disappear under the dining room archway.

Charlotte sweeps her gaze across the room, her mind still drifting between the goodbyes and the bonds formed. Then she spots Jaxson. He's over in the corner with Isabell, his giant hands cupping her cheeks so gently, as though she were something fragile. They're close, heads bowed together, exchanging words Charlotte can't hear. Whatever he's saying is meant only for her.

Isabell's laughter rings out, light and quick, and she slaps Jaxson's chest playfully before disappearing into his arms. The size difference between them is almost startling —Isabell's petite frame all but swallowed by Jaxson's hulking form. Yet, there's something incredibly tender in the way he holds her, his arms wrapping around her as though he's protecting something precious.

It's a friendship Charlotte doesn't fully understand but knows she doesn't need to. Whatever they've built is theirs —special, unspoken, and strong. A connection that runs deeper than words, rooted in something only they share. And, in this moment, watching the two of them, she can feel the quiet power of that bond.

A pang of something stirs in her chest, but she quickly pushes it aside. Not every bond has to be explained. Some just are.

In the foyer, the echoes of goodbyes bounce off the high walls, filling the space with a mix of voices and laughter that feels heavy with finality. Charlotte stands still, absorbing it all. There's a sadness swirling in the air, one that isn't entirely her own. She glances around until her eyes land on Harper, who is pressed against the wall, locked in a fervent kiss with Lucas.

Charlotte sighs, her heart tugging at the sight. She moves toward Spencer, her expression serious. "We need to figure that out," she says softly, tipping her head toward the couple. Harper's hands cling to Lucas as if letting go would mean more than just saying goodbye.

Spencer watches them for a beat, then nods. "We'll talk about it as a pack on the way home," he says. "I don't want to lose my most trusted, and I know you don't either, but we can't keep them apart. If we try, we'll lose them anyway."

He's right, and Charlotte knows it. Keeping them apart would tear them both in ways that neither pack could mend. "What if they go between the packs?" she suggests.

Spencer chuckles lightly, the tension easing just a bit. "Like shared custody?"

"Maybe." Charlotte shrugs. "Talk to Lucas, and I'll bring it up to Harper. Right now, I just want to make her happy."

Charlotte watches the exchange between Lucas and Harper, their bond palpable in every glance, every touch. But suddenly, something shifts. Lucas, with a heavy breath, quickly breaks their kiss, the warmth between them disappearing as if a cord has been snapped. His jaw clenches as he pushes off the wall, his movements tense and hurried. Without a word, he bends down, grabs his bag from the floor, and stomps toward the large front doors.

Harper stands there, frozen for a moment, her lips still parted as if his kiss lingers, her wide eyes locked on him. But she doesn't move. Her chest rises and falls unevenly, her hands hovering in the air where they had just been holding onto him moments ago.

"Lucas," she whispers, her voice barely audible, the pain clear in the way she says his name, like she's grasping at the last thread that connects them.

Lucas doesn't turn back. The tension radiates from him, his body tight with the weight of the goodbye he clearly doesn't want to make. His steps are heavy, deliberate, each one dragging him farther from her. The door slams shut behind him, echoing through the foyer like the sound of something breaking.

Luna is by Harper's side in an instant, wrapping her arms around her in comfort, but Harper's eyes stay glued to the door. "I didn't even get to say goodbye," she whispers, her voice cracking, the pain raw in every syllable.

Charlotte's heart aches watching the scene unfold. The pack bond is being stretched too thin, pulling at all of them, but none feel it more acutely than Harper and Lucas. Even with the door closed, the space between them feels endless.

Spencer gives her a nod, his respect for Charlotte clear. "We'll figure it out."

"Yeah. It needs to be fast."

Nearby, Kai's voice breaks the moment. "Wow! That picture is awesome!" He's staring at a gold-framed painting on the wall, a playful grin on his face.

Luna dances over to him, tucking herself under his arm. "That is a Luna original," she declares proudly.

Kai chuckles and pulls her closer, gazing at the painting of a field of cartoonish, brightly colored mushrooms—*dickshrooms*, as they call them. "Of course it is, beautiful," he says, planting a kiss on her forehead. "But I'm going to be too far away for any more booty calls, so I guess this is it."

Luna laughs, slapping his ass playfully. "It was fun while it lasted, stud." She winks at him before bouncing over to where Harper sits, looking utterly defeated.

As the goodbyes end, Charlotte closes the massive wrought iron door behind Spencer's final wave. Light bursts through the stained glass, casting rainbows across the marble floor, but the colors do nothing to lift the heaviness.

Charlotte feels it too, the weight of Harper's emotions settling over the room like a thick fog, touching everyone. Her inner beast, usually driven by anger, stirs restlessly inside her, howling in frustration at the raw pain flooding the space. The instinct to protect, to fix, surges through Charlotte, but there's nothing she can do to ease the heartbreak right now.

Jade stomps around the corner, breaking the silence. Without warning, she tosses something at Harper. The bundle hits her in the face before she even has time to react.

"What smells like Lucas?" Harper mumbles, grabbing the item and pulling it to her nose. She buries her face in the fabric, her expression softening for the first time as recognition dawns. "His hoodie?"

Jade leans casually against the newel post, picking at her nails, a smug smirk tugging at the corner of her mouth. "What? He left his bag open... sorta," she says with a shrug, clearly pleased with herself for the not-so-subtle theft.

Harper pulls the navy blue hoodie over her head, the white lettering on the side barely visible as she sinks into it. "Oh my god, Jade," she mutters, her voice muffled through the hoodie's softness. "I flove you. Why didn't I think to grab this?"

Jade twirls her keys around her finger, the clinking the only sound for a brief moment. "Let's go, then," she says, her tone light, though concern flickers in her eyes as she watches Harper.

Luna bounces over, cutting through the tension with her usual energy. She knocks into Jade with a playful hip bump. "Yay!" she squeals, her exuberance lifting the mood, as always.

"Luna, you don't even know where we're going," Liam says as he stands, stretching his full height.

Luna spins with a wide grin, her energy contagious. "I don't care! I'll be with my pack. Plus, this will be our first outing—just pack, with our new king." She glances at Charlotte, her eyes bright with excitement. "There will be drinks, right? Please tell me there will be drinks."

"There are drinks," Jade says, patting Luna's head. "I called Willamena. She said we could take her suite at the Knights' game this afternoon. Faceoff is in an hour, and we have to get across town, so let's go, troops."

THE TEXT

I t's been a week since the Humboldts went home.

The video call between Charlotte, Harper, Spencer, and Lucas worked out the details for Harper and Lucas' dual-pack allegiance. Both Lucas and Harper reluctantly agreed to step down from their Beta responsibilities. Jade stepped up as Beta for the Red Rocks, and a wolf named Ryan is now the Humboldt Beta.

They decided Lucas would come to Vegas for the first month. With Ethan's lingering threat, they figured extra claws here was the smarter choice.

The Cascades don't have an acting Alpha. The pack is already in chaos, and it'll only get worse. Charlotte feels for the innocents in that pack. Miles' incarceration ensures no one can challenge for Alpha, but he's still alive, which means a new Alpha can't step into the role. The pack bonds will start to rot, and havoc will follow.

Harper bounces into the game room, shaking Charlotte from her thoughts. "He'll be here in about five hours!" She plops down next to Charlotte on the sectional. "I've made room in the closet and bought new his-and-hers towels."

"Seriously? I already have to get used to 'Second Alpha,' and now I have to listen to all the lovey-kissy stuff from you two?" Jade throws a soft-tip dart, hitting the double eighteen. "Shit!"

"Fuck you, Jade. I was talking to Char, not you."

Charlotte adjusts the blanket on her lap. "And Jade, stop with the Second Alpha crap. It's just annoying. He's fine being called Liam."

Right on cue, Liam struts into the room. "Oh, I don't know, Alpha, I kind of like it."

"Well, shit. Now I need to come up with something else. I can't have you like it." Jade shoots him a wink.

But suddenly the air changes, something dark and fierce pressing down on the room. Charlotte can almost see black smoke swirling around her. The look on Liam's face tells her he feels it too. Her eyes whip to Harper. Harper's face is shifting, her wolf pushing to the surface.

"Harper, what the hell?" Charlotte grabs the phone from Harper's hand. The screen shows Lucas—bound and gagged, both eyes swollen shut, blood pooling on the floor beneath him. He's breathing, but barely.

The only words on the screen are:

"We will trade. Williams for Barlowe."

REVENGE

OF THE DESERT WOLF

Red Rock Series
Book 2

JD WOLFE

"REVENGE OF THE DESERT WOLF"

Harper Sheridan is known for being the level-headed one, always approaching problems with a clear mind and logical solutions. Finally finding her mate after giving up hope, she's eager to start their new life of dual-pack allegiance as Lucas makes his way to join her.

But everything changes when she receives a message from their enemy. The desert will run red with her revenge.

Meanwhile, Lucas wakes in an unfamiliar place, his body broken and on the brink of death, with no memory of how he got there. Endless questions plague his mind as he struggles to piece together the truth of what happened— and who he really is.

As the packs race to find Lucas, they also face growing pressure from the Council as long-hidden secrets come to light.

In *Revenge of the Desert Wolf*, author JD Wolfe delivers a heart-pounding tale of loyalty, love, revenge, and the unbreakable bonds of family.